I found the right paper and folded it back. "January 30, New Jersey Pick-Six..." I looked. Then I stared and matched up my ticket with the paper: 4, 7... My eyes leaped back and forth and my heart went *blump, blump, blump, blump.* 4, 7, 14, 18, 33, 37. I looked once again, with my mouth hanging open. The numbers were identical. I let out a howl: *"Aaaaaiiiieeee!"*

My mom looked at me. "Very funny."

"Let *me* see." My dad took the ticket and the newspaper calmly. I can't tell you how loud my second howl was when he said, "My God, Mary, he won."

UNEASY
Money

ROBIN F. BRANCATO

BORZOI SPRINTERS · ALFRED A. KNOPF
New York

DR. M. JERRY WEISS, Distinguished Service Professor of Communications at Jersey City State College, is the educational consultant for Borzoi Sprinters. A past chair of the International Reading Association President's Advisory Committee on Intellectual Freedom, he travels frequently to give workshops on the use of trade books in schools.

A BORZOI SPRINTER PUBLISHED BY ALFRED A. KNOPF, INC.

Copyright © 1986 by Robin F. Brancato

Cover art copyright © 1989 by John Zielinski

All rights reserved under International and Pan-American Copyright Conventions. Published in the United States by Alfred A. Knopf, Inc., New York, and simultaneously in Canada by Random House of Canada Limited, Toronto. Distributed by Random House, Inc., New York. Originally published by Alfred A. Knopf, Inc., as a Borzoi Book in 1986.

Library of Congress Catalog Card Number: 86-45296

ISBN: 0-394-82055-X

RL: 5.5

First Borzoi Sprinter edition: June 1989

Manufactured in the United States of America

0 1 2 3 4 5 6 7 8 9

For Tessie and her sons

UNEASY
Money

Picture this. A comic strip with four frames. In the first frame you see a guy in bed, sleeping. He looks something like me—fairly big build, decent face, hard-to-keep-neat light brown hair. He's *enjoying* sleeping, really into it—there's a line of Z's coming out of his mouth. Meanwhile his parents are yelling at him from downstairs. What they're saying is in huge print: "GET UP, MIKE! CLEAN YOUR ROOM! BRING DOWN YOUR LAUNDRY! TAKE THOSE NEWSPAPERS OUT!"

In frame two he's sleeping deeper—he obviously hasn't heard a word.

Okay, frame three: His mom winks at his dad and whispers (in tiny little print), "Do you think we should buy Mike a car, now that he's eighteen?"

Frame four: Mike leaps out of bed, runs down the stairs in his Jockey shorts, and stands breathless in front of his parents. "Did you say something?" he asks.

Dumb idea for a comic strip? I know it. That's why I decided not to draw it as I lay in bed on that bleak first Sunday morning in February, five months ago. I'd been

3

lying there for a while, half awake, hoping for comic inspiration, but nothing seemed funny—not after my argument with Sheila the night before and after losing thirty bucks to Barry DeVane.

"Mike! Did you hear me? How about bringing your laundry down?"

That was the real voice of my mother, but before I could answer, a flying object zinged through the air and just missed my head. "Hey!" I sat up.

My one and only sibling Amy, in the doorway, wound up and threw again. "You left them in the bathroom," she said, referring to my sneakers. "When are you going to stop being a slob?"

"Never." I grinned. Amy and I are locked in this battle of wits, and since she's usually away at college, when she's home once in a while on weekends we have to make every battling minute count. I looked at her then and saw she was skinnier, if such a thing was possible. The way she hardly eats anything drives my mom and grandmother nuts. "When did *you* get home?" I asked her.

"Last night. I got a ride, and I thought I could study better here."

"You came all the way home just to study?"

"That's what some of us go to school for." At this point she looked around at the wreck of my room.

The mess was intentional, actually. I had been doing these still lifes, let's call them—sketches of things in my room, with titles like "Pile of College Catalogs and Overdue Library Books, with Sweat Socks and Twinkie Wrappers."

"Mother lets you live like this?" Amy asked me.

"Yeah," I said. "I'm her favorite kid."

Amy came into the room then and looked at me pityingly. Especially since she's been taking psychology, she sees deep meaning in everything. "You think you're joking, but it's true—mothers often prefer their sons. Too bad you aren't acquainted with what Sigmund Freud said."

I put on a German accent. "Yah, yah, last time I talked to Freud, he said, 'Dot Amy's a mental case!'" Then I reached for one of my sneakers and threw it.

She stepped aside so that it missed her. "You're regressing," she said. "Eighteen and you act like you're ten."

She was making one of those disgusted faces that spoils her otherwise good looks. I've often drawn caricatures of her like that—long dark hair tossed back, eyebrows arched, and lips sort of puckered up, as if she's just bitten into an apple and noticed half a worm.

Then she happened to glance at the pile of college catalogs on my desk and her expression changed. "Have you applied anywhere yet?" she asked me with real interest.

This protective-big-sister thing was another side of Amy that came through every once in a while. I had a hard time adjusting to her changes, though, so I wasn't as appreciative as I should have been. "So far I only sent out two applications," I told her. "One to this *inferior* place . . ."

"Where?"

"Murray State." That's where Amy goes. Murray's probably as good as any other New Jersey school—I just said that to get her going.

"Well, you're right that it isn't Harvard," she said. "Are you applying anywhere else?"

"Yeah, I already did, to Cummings Institute in California. Ron Schwartz applied there too. It's a school of commercial art near Los Angeles."

"Mother and Daddy are *letting* you go to a school in California?"

She was back to being Amy the Pain again. "They don't know it yet, actually," I told her. "Don't say anything, okay? I figure maybe if I get in, they'll break down and say yes."

"They'd better not," Amy said. "I wanted to go to school out-of-state in the worst way, but Daddy insisted the state colleges were all we could afford."

"Take it easy, take it easy. They'll probably shoot me down too. If I get in, that is—if Cummings decides they like my work."

"That's *work*?" Her eyes shifted to my drawing board, where there was a bunch of cartoons spread out. Amy picked one up and studied it. "You did this?" she said. "Not bad."

I smiled modestly, but all of a sudden I swallowed my smile. "Wait, that one Ron did," I admitted. Ron Schwartz is my oldest and best friend. We go back to the fourth grade.

"I thought this was too political for you," Amy said. She's right, I'm not political. I've been cartooning since I was a kid, but I just draw simple everyday things. I guess "Doonesbury" and some of those other political strips are good—I wouldn't mind having the success of Garry Trudeau—but I think if you're going to put that many words in a comic, you may as well write a book. At that point I handed Amy one of my recent cartoons, one that showed a guy sneaking into his bedroom late at night by climbing up the drainpipe.

"Sophomoric," she said. "By the way"—she looked up—"where were you so late last night? I heard you come in at three or four o'clock."

"Over at Barry's," I said, referring to Barry DeVane, my friend who has his own apartment. "We were debating the nuclear issue and completely lost track of time." I cackled. "Just kidding, Ames, old girl. We were deep into poker. How about it, could you lend me thirty bucks until next week?"

She put on her disgusted face again. "I live in abject poverty, on a minimal allowance, and you're asking to borrow from *me* to pay off a poker debt? What do you do with what Mother and Daddy give you? And I thought you were working."

"Yeah, fifteen hours a week, but it's expensive to live."

"The way *you* must live, sure. We just got money for Christmas, and didn't Grandma give you her usual on your birthday? What do you spend your money on?"

"Food, I'm a growing boy. Movies, tapes, more food, taking Sheila out . . ."

Amy reacted as if I'd just said the dirtiest of dirty words. "You always pay when you go out with Sheila?"

"Yeah."

"Aren't you being terribly macho? Doesn't Sheila resent it?"

"Nope." I grinned evilly. "She likes real men." The truth was I wished Sheila would pay sometimes, but she's kind of old-fashioned. Right then she was probably waiting for *me* to call *her*, to apologize for the night before.

"Mike! The laundry!" my mom yelled again.

"Yeah!" I shouted, and the mattress started shaking. I'd woken up Muttsy, our dog, who sleeps under my bed.

"Hi, Muttsy baby! Come to Amy," she coaxed, but Muttsy jumped in bed with me.

Amy looked hurt and I didn't blame her. Muttsy used to be mainly her dog. Amy pretended she didn't care, by casually walking out of my room. "No thirty-buck loan?" I called, not so much to tease her as to try to bring her back. That's the thing—Amy bugs me, but I feel like something's missing when she goes away.

Her voice echoed down the hall: "You're out of your mind!"

"Wait a minute," I tried again. "It's not for a poker debt, it's for one of your organizations!" Amy's into all these *causes*. "It's for"—I strained my twisted brain—"Starving Deaf Mutes Against—*Pornography*!"

Amy came back and stuck her head in the door. "If you have to mock *me*, go ahead, but don't mock deprived and disabled people. What I spend *my* time on does some good, at least."

"I wasn't mocking them!" I said impatiently. "I'm just saying quit being so hung up on serious stuff. Can't you enjoy life?"

"The organizations I'm involved with at school *are* what I enjoy." She trotted off again down the hall. "And no radios or stereos!" she called back to me. "I can't deal with being disturbed today. I've got a major test coming up."

I made a quick trip to the bathroom with Muttsy trailing me as usual. She dogs my footsteps, as they say, whenever I'm home. Amy and I found Muttsy on the street about ten years ago. It's as if Mutts knows she lost her owner once and follows me everywhere to make sure it won't happen again.

I came back from the bathroom with the hamper and put on a pair of jeans and a torn sweatshirt, and while Muttsy licked cream filling from some stray Twinkie wrappers, I slowly picked up my dirty clothes. Then I carried the hamper downstairs, with Muttsy hot on my heels.

"Well!" My mom was perched at the table, finishing a

cup of tea. "Finally—the prince is honoring us with his presence."

"Some prince." My dad put down his paper and looked up from his scrambled eggs. "Dressed in his royal robes. What time did you come in last night?"

"Not that late," I said, glad that Amy wasn't there to testify against me.

"Where were you?"

"Barry's."

"Who else was over there?" my dad asked.

"Ronnie and Lingo."

"What do you *do* when you go to Barry's?" my mom asked, handing me a glass of orange juice.

I hated the third degree I'd been getting from them lately. "Oh, listen to music, play cards." Naturally I didn't mention losing my shirt.

"You can bring your friends here, you know," she said.

My dad gave her his are-you-kidding? look. "They don't want to be where any parents are!"

He was right about that. Not that the four of us were doing anything so awful, but who needed adults breathing down our necks? My dad got going at that point on the subject of the freedom kids have today, but I wasn't listening. In my mind I was drawing a cartoon kid with one parent breathing down his neck and the other on his back. The breather looked like my dad, complete with bald spot, and the dark eyebrows that Amy inherited, and the chipmunk jowls he's developed lately from eating a little too much. Perched on the kid's back—or on his shoulder, rather—was a birdlike mom something like my mom—with a face like an older Princess Diana and some worry lines around her eyes. I drew the dad with a lopsided smile to indicate he was moody but not really a bad guy, and the mom whispering in the kid's ear, as if she was trying to be his conscience.

Would I draw this one on paper? Yeah, if I had time. Would I show it to my parents? Maybe my mom, but not my dad. He used to show off my cartoons at work when I was little, when he thought drawing was just a nice hobby, but since I've been saying I want to be a cartoonist? Forget it—he's into *security*. My dad himself has worked twenty-some years selling commercial real estate for the same company. My mom wants me to work at something I like, but she's also basically practical. She'd be totally satisfied if I ended up teaching art in the school where she teaches second grade. Just to give an idea of how adventurous my parents are—their idea of a big risk is buying a whole book of raffles on PTA College Night.

Anyway, while I was still pretending to draw them, they started hounding me about my math grades, so that I thought of certain animated cartoons I'd seen where the artist uses his power. I mean the kind of cartoon where Tom and Jerry do something really obnoxious, let's say, and you see the hand of the artist erasing them. My parents had better be careful, I thought, or I'd erase them on the spot.

That's where my head was just then, as we finished our breakfast and my mom, dragging the hamper into the laundry room, asked me if I was going to church. "I'm thinking about it!" I called. We're officially Catholic, but only my mom and I ever go. My dad says the church just wants your money and my sister Amy's an atheist.

"Before you go anywhere"—my dad got up—"you have some obligations around here. I need a hand with some stuff in the basement and those newspapers have to go out."

I looked up lazily. "I thought Sunday was supposed to be a day of rest."

He swatted me with his newspaper. "Every day is a day of rest for you!"

I smiled and sat back. If you ask me, he's a workaholic. He and Amy—neither of them can sit still. Lately he'd been knocking himself out all day and then coming home and working at his desk at night. At least my mom's a little more like me—she's not as uptight about neatness, and she relaxes in the evening and enjoys sleeping a lot.

One more word about my family—have I made them sound awful? My dad a tyrant, my mom a nag, my sister Amy a pain in the butt? The fact is, I wouldn't trade 'em. It's not just that being an orphan would be lonely— who would provide me with material for "The Family Circus"-type cartoons I like to draw?

At that point, as I got up, my mom came back into the kitchen. "All this would have ended up in the washing machine if I hadn't gone through your pockets," she said. She dropped a handful of stuff on the table—a pack of gum, a comb, a ticket. "What's that, a lottery ticket?"

"Yeah."

"Since when do you buy those?" my dad asked.

"I bought one on my birthday. I figured maybe I'd get lucky."

"And?"

"I don't know. I forgot to check it."

"The kid has money to throw away."

"What do you mean," I protested. "The lottery money goes for education in New Jersey."

My dad elbowed me. "I'd rather see you doing your bit for education by hitting the books."

"Better watch it," I reminded him, "I'm bigger than you

now." Just barely, but I notice lately when he bawls me out, he waits till we're both sitting down.

"Let me check the number," I said, partly to put off doing the basement cleanup. "It should be in Friday's paper—where is it?"

"In the closet, with the others, waiting for you to take them out."

I went and rooted through the pile. While my dad waited impatiently, I flipped pages. "Hold it, wait—here." I found the right paper and folded it back. "January 30, New Jersey Pick-Six . . ." I looked. Then I stared and matched up my ticket with the paper: 4, 7 . . . My eyes leaped back and forth and my heart went *blump, blump, blump, blump*. 4, 7, 14, 18, 33, 37. I looked once again, with my mouth hanging open. The numbers were identical. I let out a howl: *"Aaaaaiiiieeee!"*

My mom looked at me. "Very funny."

I shoved the ticket and newspaper at her. She's lived through years of my horsing around, so I didn't blame her for wanting proof. While I jiggled with excitement and fear that I'd been seeing things, she was trying like mad to read the numbers without her glasses.

"Let *me* see." My dad took the ticket and the newspaper from her calmly. I can't tell you how loud my second howl was when he said, "My God, Mary, he won."

2

During the first couple of minutes after we'd discovered my winning number, the three of us kept pulling the newspaper out of each other's hands. "Let me see again!" "Unbelievable!" "Hahaheee! I'm rich!" Then we all started talking at once and Muttsy began barking. Finally my dad, sweat glistening on his forehead, raised his hand for silence. "Wait. Wait a minute. Are you sure this ticket's good?"

"Yeah, I bought it on my birthday, Monday. I'm positive."

"How much is it worth?"

When I shrugged, he grabbed the paper again and turned from page to page.

"Wait, here it is, here it is . . . my God—$2,407,238—almost two and a half million dollars." Dropping the paper, he stared at my mom and then at me. "Are you absolutely sure it's good?"

"Good as gold. I bought it at Freddy's." Freddy's is a candy and newspaper store right near my school. This other guy ahead of me had asked for a ticket and I had said, "Hey, Freddy, I'm legal today—eighteen—I'll take one, too!"

"Tell Amy," my mom said suddenly. "Get Amy. Amy!"

Naturally Amy didn't even answer. She's worse than I am about coming when she's called. We yelled in unison a few times, and then Muttsy and I charged upstairs.

"Mike, I'll kill you," she said, her nose in a book. "I'm doing statistics! What do you *want* from me?"

I was half jumping out of my skin. "Come down and find out. Come down, I'll make it worth your while." When she still didn't move, I came up behind her, pulled her off her chair, and got her into a fireman's carry that I'd learned in lifesaving class.

"Put me down!" She struggled. "Quit manhandling me! I'll *come*! What's *wrong* with him?" she called to our parents, who were waiting at the bottom of the stairs.

"Tell her," my dad urged me as I set Amy down.

"*Tell* her, Mike!" my mom begged.

The four of us stood in the downstairs hallway, and I crossed my hands over my heart. "No lying, Ames, old girl, I just won two and a half million bucks."

Amy rolled her eyes, as she often does. "What's this, early April Fools' Day? Thanks a lot for your understanding. I've got a statistics exam tomorrow!"

I showed her the evidence, but even then it took time until it sank in. Finally, when it did, she said, "Of all people—*Mike*!"

I let her remark pass for the time being, because at that point the four of us looked at each other and then, as if being pulled by a magnet, we moved into a huddle, locked arms, and started swaying like little kids. We hadn't done anything like that, I thought, for ten years at least. Finally we broke apart, still laughing, with Muttsy running around nipping our ankles.

My mom sat down, out of breath. "How'd you pick the numbers?"

"Different ones in my life—our address, and my age, and the last two I just picked out of the air."

My dad paced with a dazed expression. "What do we do now?"

Amy couldn't sit either. She was hugging herself as if she was cold. "I can't get *over* it," she said. "It's so ironic that *you* won."

"Why?"

"I mean *you*, who can't keep track of one week's allowance!"

"Are you saying I don't deserve it?"

"Not exactly, it's just that—"

"I think this is just what Mike needs," my mom broke in.

"Oh boy, oh boy," my dad murmured, "what a way to learn money management!"

"The best," I agreed. "What do you all want to buy?"

"One thing at a time," my dad said. "How do you file the claim?"

"I think you go where you bought the ticket."

"Call up and ask."

I picked up the wall phone over the table, got the number from information, and had a quick conversation with Freddy at Freddy's News.

"What did he say?" They all pounced on me.

"Freddy knew he had a winner. It's all mine!" I exploded. "I'm the only Pick-Six winner this week. He's been waiting since yesterday for somebody to call. I have to get in touch with the Lottery Commission in Trenton first thing tomorrow and then go down there with the ticket and they'll give me my check."

"Trenton?" "Tomorrow?" While they were gabbing and asking more questions, I was asking myself some. Who should I tell first? What should I buy?

"Call Ma," I heard my dad say.

"Yeah, Grandma." I reached for the phone, but when I dialed, there was no answer. "I'm calling Ronnie," I told them. "He was with me when—"

"Hold it." My dad held up his hand. "Let's get used to this idea ourselves for a couple of minutes before we let the whole world in on it." He went to the closet where the papers were and came back with a bottle of champagne. "This isn't cold"—he took a towel and popped open the bottle—"but we'll put it in orange juice. Glasses, Mary?" He poured. "Isn't it amazing how quick things can change in this life?"

Yeah, I thought, and how. Fifteen minutes before they'd been on my back, now they were celebrating and pouring me champagne. This was cartoon stuff—a kid's broke, he pulls his pockets inside out and they're empty, and then in the next frame hundred-dollar bills are raining down on his head.

"Look what time it is!" my mom said suddenly. "We were going to go to church, and now it's too late."

My dad filled her glass again. "Don't worry about it. They'll be even happier to see Mike there next week, after he gets his check."

I myself was glad to stay just where I was, letting the incredible news sink in.

"Let's have a toast." My mom got up. She looked giddy, very unusual for her. "May Mike have health, wealth, and wisdom." She raised her glass. "Make that mainly *health.*"

Now my dad held his glass up. *"Cin-cin!"* That's Italian for "cheers!" Dad's never been to Italy, but he's proud of his roots. "Here's to the first millionaire in the Bronti family, and every penny of it legal!" He can't stand when people think *Mafia* just because someone's got an Italian name.

"My turn," Amy said, her voice very emotional. "Some people say—I'm sure you've heard it—you can't be too skinny or too rich."

I looked at her cross-eyed. "Who said that, Freud?"

"No, Gloria Vanderbilt, or somebody. But I don't agree necessarily. I don't think you can be too skinny, but some people are too rich. Here's my toast: To Mike—may this money make him a good person."

"Hey, what do you mean—I'm a bad person now?"

"Not *bad.*" She tilted her head. "What I mean is, with this money I hope you'll do really big things."

Yeah? For the first time in a long time, I didn't argue with Amy. Doing big things with my money was exactly what I had in mind.

3

"Try Grandma again," my parents suggested.

I dialed, but there was still no answer. "I'm calling Ron now," I said, and I finally sat down. I was feeling charged, I remember, as if electrical wires were under my skin, and it was hard to sit still while I dialed the phone.

"The Schwartz residence," a tinny voice said, "home of Jack and Sylvia and their gifted son, Irwin Ronald. If you wish to leave a message for Ronald, please wait for the tone . . ."

"Cool it, Ron, it's *me.*" The Schwartzes don't even have an answering machine. That routine is just something Ron does to amuse himself.

He made a rude noise he uses only with me. "Hey, Bronti, what's happening?"

"Are you sitting down?" I asked him. "Are you ready to hear something big?"

"Give it to me straight, man. I can take it standing up."

I could picture him in his crazy bedroom, surrounded by the murals he's painted, "X-Man" on one wall and "Tales of the Crypt" on the other. "Listen," I went on, "remem-

18

ber Freddy's on Monday? I bought a lottery ticket, remember?"

"Don't tell me you got lucky. What'd you win?"

"Guess."

"Forty bucks."

"Guess again."

"Okay—you hit the jackpot."

"Yeah." I waited, holding my breath. Meanwhile my family was listening and laughing. Ron was silent, completely silent. "I'm serious," I said. He's known me long enough to tell whether I'm kidding or not. The next thing I heard was—

"*Arrrrggggghhh!* When did you find out?"

"Just now when my mom found the ticket. You're the first one to know it. Think you could round up Barry and Lingo and come over in a little while?"

"Yeah!"

"Let me tell them myself, though."

"You mean don't say anything, just bring them over? Okay, Michael Bigbucks, sir. At your service. See you then." He paused for a second, and I could almost hear his brainwaves crackling. "This means the ultimate Bronti-Schwartz fantasy can be a reality sooner than we thought!"

He was referring to this plan we'd had since fifth grade or something, of the two of us having our own Disneyland-type amusement park. "Nothing to stop us now," I told him.

He let out a gleeful sound. "Your money and my brains! That's all it'll take! See you later."

Hanging up the phone and seeing my family there watching me, I guess it really hit me for the first time: KID CARTOONIST COPS CASH, STRUGGLING TEEN HITS WINNING

STREAK. Nothing like this had ever happened before. Amy was right, it *was* pretty funny. After eighteen years of being like a kid in Santa's lap, suddenly I was Santa himself! "What does everyone want?" I asked them again.

"To go to Africa," Amy answered.

"*Africa*," my mom repeated. "Amy, can't you think of someplace *farther away*?"

I jumped to Amy's defense. "Let her do what she wants! Africa—you got it. Mom, you want a vacation? You want to buy a new house?"

"I love *this* house," my mom said. "Why should I move?"

"For some excitement, to do something different. What about you, Dad? Quit your job!"

"And live off you for the rest of my life?" He laughed.

Just then the doorbell rang and we looked at each other. Muttsy charged at the door and I followed her. I opened it. "Hey, Grandma! Hi, wow, wait'll you hear!"

"I went to early mass," she said in a rush, tilting her face so I could kiss her. "And when I got home I thought, I feel like going over there. I'm no stranger that I got to call first, am I right?"

"Who is it? Hi, Ma!" By now my parents and Amy were welcoming Grandma.

"You couldn't have picked a better time," I told her. "Here, let me take that." I unloaded her shopping bag and her coat. "We've got big news—"

"Amy's home!" Grandma pushed past me. "I just barge in without calling! And here's the big guy," she said, standing on her toes to kiss my dad. "Some Catholic I raised him to be. Mary, you didn't go to church either, today? Shame on you." Kissing all of us on our cheeks, she left bright red marks.

"We tried to call you, Ma," my dad said.

"We have big news, Grandma," I said again.

"Bad news? I had a feeling!"

"*Big* news," I repeated. Her hearing's not that good. Meanwhile my dad steered her into the kitchen and sat her down in a chair.

"How big, that I have to sit down? Should I take one of my pills first? Mike, leave those cutlets out. I cooked 'em this morning to eat now in sandwiches. I know"—she settled herself in the chair—"Amy met a boy."

"No!" Amy groaned.

"It's Mike's news," my mom said.

My dad nudged me. "For God's sake, will you tell her?"

"You know the lottery, Grandma? The one where you pick six numbers, one through forty-six?"

"The lottery, yeah. My hairdresser won a couple hundred dollars."

I sucked in my breath. "I won a lot more than that. Two and a half million bucks."

"Million?" Her eyes were big circles, like Little Orphan Annie eyes. "The number two, and then I don't know how many little zeroes?" She grabbed me and pulled down my head and gave me another kiss. "Go away, Mutts," she said, laughing as Muttsy tried to come between us. "So Mike's a winner! I knew someday . . . where is it?" she asked suddenly.

"The ticket?"

"The money!"

I made my face deadpan. "They delivered it a little while ago, in nickels. That's what we were doing when you came, filling up drawers."

"You're kidding me." She let out a hoot and gave me a bear hug. "Your grandpa, may he rest in peace, used to kid

me like that. Mike's just like his grandpa. I don't believe
one word he says."

"It's true that he won, Ma," my dad told her evenly.
"He has to call Trenton tomorrow and then go down and
get a check."

She clung to my dad. "Okay, I believe it when Lou tells
me. He doesn't kid. It's good there's one in the family I can
trust. Wait till the girls in my club hear. Your grandpa'd
die if he knew it! Oh, listen how dumb I talk. He's been
gone eleven years! I never won nothing myself." She
reached over and squeezed me. "Two million! You still
gonna talk to us beggars?"

"Sure, Grandma. You won't be beggars long. What do
you want?"

"Let me see." She sat back and folded her arms over her
chest. "A new fur coat—that animal I been wearing looks
like he died of a skin disease."

"You want it, you got it! Nothing's too good for
Grandma!" I said. For fifteen years she'd been slipping
Amy and me tens under the table. Now it would be *my*
turn. What an incredible switch.

"What are we waiting for?" my grandma asked. "When
you're happy, you got to celebrate. And when you celebrate, you eat. Bring me that shopping bag, Mike. There's
cutlets and pepperoni, and look at this Italian bread—"

"I have a roast in the oven, Ma," my mother told her.

"You'll have the roast tonight." She unpacked the bag.

"I wasn't going to eat today," Amy said.

"What are you, crazy? You look like a spaghetti already!
Poor people or millionaires, you still got to eat." Grandma
was sawing away, slicing the bread, when the doorbell
rang a second time. "Who's that? You're expecting somebody?"

"Get the door, Mike," my dad said.

When I opened this time, a man said, "Hello, I'm from Channel Thirty. Are you Mike Bronti?"

"Yes—"

"I'm John Kosikowski, producer-director. I'm here with my assistants, Ann Hadley, reporter, and cameraman Jerry Pardeau. We got your name and address from Freddy's News. Congratulations." He shook my hand. "We tried to call you before we came over, but your line was occupied. We hope you'll let us do an interview . . ."

By this time my whole family had gathered in the doorway. Muttsy was yapping, and as soon as my grandma understood who it was, she started putting on lipstick and combing her hair. "Come in," I told John. The van outside said GLENFIELD CHANNEL 30, LOCAL NEWS ALL THE TIME.

"Do we want them to do this . . . ?" My mom looked skeptical, and so did my father.

"Sure, no problem," I told them, and to Kosikowski, "Come on in."

Jerry lugged in the cameras. Ann, the reporter, petted Muttsy, and John began sizing up the location and talking to my mom.

"Nice place," he said, "very homey. You've lived here a long time?"

"Nineteen years." My mom was won over, now that he had complimented the house.

To me our house is okay—it's all brick and on a nice street and everything, but it's not so terrific that you'd want to stay in it if you got rich. Here in Glenfield almost everybody lives about the same—no shacks and no mansions. I like Glenfield basically, but sometimes it's a little dull.

John and Jerry, who were setting up meanwhile, decided the kitchen had the best light, so they arranged us around the table, as if we were about to eat. They asked my grandma to slice bread, and they wanted my mom to be serving food. "Don't make us look like a Ronzoni commercial!" my dad complained, so John agreed that we should all be standing up, looking at the ticket.

"We're in the kitchen of 4714 Court Street, Glenfield," Ann began with the cameras rolling, "in the home of Mike Bronti, New Jersey's latest and youngest lottery millionaire. How does it feel, Mike?"

"Wow." I smiled hard to make up for not having anything brilliant to say.

"Mary Bronti"—Ann turned to my mother—"I understand you rescued the ticket from the washing machine."

"Yes—one of the many domestic crises I deal with every day."

"And how do you feel, Mr. Louis Bronti, father of the winner? Is Mike a chip off the old block? Are you a lottery player, too?"

"No, no," my dad said nervously, looking at the camera as if it were a machine gun. "I'm one of those guys who tried to teach my kid that gambling doesn't pay."

Ann seemed to think that was funny, and my dad smiled in relief, as if the machine gun had turned out to be only a camera after all.

Then Ann moved on to my grandma. "Anna Bronti, the family matriarch . . . How does it feel to be the grandmother of a teenage millionaire?"

"He's a good boy. He deserves it. He never did a mean thing to nobody . . ."

Grandma defends the family automatically, whether we're being attacked or not. She finished by wiping lipstick off my cheek. "There! *I* did that before, when I kissed him." Then she looked into the camera. "Can I say hello? Hi, Lena, Margaret, Tess! How are you, girls?"

My dad was enjoying it, I was glad to see. Sometimes Grandma embarrasses him, but with this wave of luck hitting us, how could anybody be annoyed?

Next came Amy. "What do *you* think, Amy Bronti, Mike's older sister, a college sophomore . . . ?"

Amy's lips curled in a strange smile. "I think he'll spend the money well."

Hey, hey, how about that—Amy, my sibling rival, was finally saying something nice about me!

"Thank you, Amy, and all of you," Ann gushed. "Mike, do you know yet what you'll do with your money?"

What could I say that other lottery winners hadn't already said? "I'm sending my sister to Africa," I began ticking off, "and paying for art school for myself, and I'll be giving the rest of my family whatever they want." I glanced at my mom, who's often my conscience, and then at Amy, who had just paid me one of her first compliments ever, and I heard myself saying, "and then I'm going to set up a fund, to support worthy causes."

"Very unusual!" Ann applauded. "Especially coming from a member of the so-called Me Generation. It looks as if Mike Bronti knows his priorities, and other people count. How can viewers get in touch with you about their causes?"

"Uh, they can write to me here—4714 Court Street, Glenfield."

"Wonderful! We'll be flashing that address on the screen, for those of you out there who would like to write to Mike. It's been a pleasure to meet Mike Bronti, New

Jersey's youngest and most generous lottery winner so far. And now to Charles Lacey and the Channel Thirty Weekend Ski Report."

I flashed a V for victory sign at the audience, and then, just before the camera stopped rolling, I called out, "It's great being a winner. Take a chance—it could happen to you!"

"That was nice," Grandma said as the TV crew left the house. "The only thing I wish—I wish I *knew*, so I'd have gone and had my hair done yesterday."

"You looked fine, Ma," my mother said. "It's going to be on sometime after two this afternoon. You'll watch it and see how good you looked, okay?"

"I don't know"—my dad shook his head as the Channel 30 van pulled out of the driveway—"putting our address on TV like that—every nut case in Glenfield knows where to find us now."

"Did you mean it, Mike?" Amy asked as we all trooped back into the kitchen. "Are you serious about giving away money, like you said?"

"Yeah."

"We've got to talk."

"Sure, anytime." This was truly amazing. Instead of me having to ask favors from Amy, she'd be having to ask me for favors from now on.

"Hold on, you two. . . ." My dad pulled out chairs for us at the table. "It sounds easy to give away money, but I guarantee you it isn't. We've got to hook you up with our

27

accountant, Mike. Meanwhile you'd better play down this giveaway program. Sure, you can give something to charity, but you aren't John D. Rockefeller—"

"Daddy," Amy protested, "Mike finally wants to *do* something good!"

"Maybe one do-gooder in the Bronti family is enough," my mom said.

"Are you sure I was *born* into this family?" Amy demanded. "Are you sure I wasn't adopted?"

My grandma stopped making sandwiches. "What's this adopted?"

Meanwhile my mom reached over and smoothed Amy's hair. "Sorry to disappoint you, honey—we're your biological parents. I mean, who would know better than I? After all, I was *there.*"

This was a discussion I'd heard before. Amy was always claiming she must have been adopted. I'd even drawn a cartoon showing Amy being hatched from a big purple egg.

"Your hair and eyes is just like Daddy's!" Grandma reminded her. "What's a matter, you don't like this family? So get married! That's what I did—only sixteen, married your grandpa just like that."

"Grandma, I have a whole lot to do first, okay?" Amy said. She turned to me without missing a beat. "I'd really like you to meet my friends from Murray African Relief."

"Come on," my dad said, "let Mike *get* his money before you wheedle it out of him for charities. Let's break out those cutlets. What we need is some Bronti Relief."

So Grandma handed around cutlet sandwiches, my mom looked at me to say grace, and even Amy forgot world starvation long enough to actually eat. There were constant interruptions, though, and this was *before* we'd told anybody. Aunt Barbara called from Texas, a friend of Amy's wanted a ride back to school. Plus, by chance, Phil Mercer, my dad's accountant, called, and my dad stayed on the phone so long that my grandma finally yelled, "Talk about that stuff tomorrow! We're having a party here!"

When my dad sat down again, Grandma got going on her family stories. No meal would be complete without a couple of Grandma's tales—some sad, like how my grandfather lost his barber shop during the Depression. But most of them were funny, like how once my grandparents were invited to this flashy party, where they were seated at the head table. Waiters kept serving them as if they were guests of honor. It was only after they got home that they realized that they'd gotten the invitation by mistake. It was supposed to have gone to a Mafia chief named Rocco "Hammerfist" Bronti.

She went on, telling mostly about how poor they were when my dad was a kid. "You think I'm going to say, 'We was poor, but oh boy, we was happy'? Forget it, we're much better off now! I love money!" She chucked my chin the way you do to a baby. "That's why I'm so happy for *this* guy!"

Everybody was happy. Man, look at them. Even my dad, who'd been pressured lately. Even Amy, with her exams and her worrying about the world. Nothing like money to set things straight. Who said money was the root of all evil? If you *stole* it, sure, but my money was *good*.

At some point, as we were finishing eating, I suddenly remembered my girlfriend, Sheila, and I was tempted to leave the table to give her a call. But my grandma wanted me there, plus I decided it might be interesting if Sheila found out about my win accidentally while she was watching TV.

I may as well say something about Sheila Cooke. We'd been going together for about three months. It started when she saw me sketching her instead of doing my graphs in math. Sheila's beautiful, let's face it. Blond. Looks like she ought to be doing shampoo ads. Anyway, she was flattered by my drawing, and when I asked her out, she said yes. Her body's great, too. Not that I've seen all of it yet, but I've got a pretty good visual imagination. I may have to be patient about seeing the rest, though—she's not the most modern girl in the world. Even our fight the night before sounds like something out of a fifties TV show—Sheila was annoyed because I was just *talking* to this person I work with, Lynne Carter.

When the phone rang at that point, I thought maybe Sheila was calling me. That's why I jumped up from the table to get it so fast. "Hello?"

"Bronti?"

"Yeah?"

"I heard about you over at Freddy's."

"Who is this?"

"Lennie. You know me, right? Lennie Thompson."

Lennie? I wracked by brain. Who did I know with a voice that sounded as if he was holding his nose?

"Lennie Thompson from North Glenfield. I'm the guy who asked for a lottery ticket ahead of you, and you said—"

"Oh, yeah, yeah, *Lennie*! Pretty strange, huh? the way things worked out!"

He cleared his throat. "Let's meet, okay? I'd like to talk to you."

"Sure—"

"When?"

"Well, I don't know. I'm going to be pretty busy. Give me your number."

"Nah, you'll forget. I'll call you back."

"Okay, do that—in a few weeks. Keep playing those numbers, Thompson, maybe it'll happen to you next. So long."

"Who was that?" my dad asked when I sat down at the table.

"Some guy I know from Freddy's—"

"Oh, boy," he said, "we'd better get an unlisted number. Can't you picture the phone ringing off the hook after they air that videotape?"

I didn't say so, but what I was thinking was, it's *about time* something was happening around here.

After we cleaned up lunch, my dad was impatient. He and my mom had agreed to drive Amy and her friend back to school. "Let's go, so I can drive while it's light," he said. "You're coming with us, Mike?"

"No, the guys are coming over." I could tell he wanted me to go—he's big on families being together on Sundays—but I didn't want to spend the first hours of my win cooped up in a car.

"You're not coming?" Amy was disappointed. "I wanted to talk to you about this project we're working on at school—"

"Tell me now." I led her away from the others into the laundry room and I shut the door. "Shoot."

"I have *so* many ideas." Amy paced in front of the washer. When she gets excited, she gets all pink-cheeked. "Have you ever thought of taking a year off?" she asked me. "Before going to college?"

I fingered the lottery ticket in my pocket. "No . . ."

She looked at me seriously, the way she used to when we were kids and she could wrap me around her finger. "Come with me to Africa in September."

"Amy," I said, not wanting to disappoint her, "I'll give you the money to go. It's not my thing right now."

Her feelings were hurt, though. "I see how it's going to be," she said. "You'll give some money away like you said, but you'll go to California. You'll get used to the good life—that is, what *most* people think is good. You'll play around in Hollywood, and get used to the climate, and marry Sheila or somebody like her—"

It all sounded pretty great to me, but I didn't say that. "I know you think I'm—"

"Frivolous," she finished. "But you have the potential not to be."

"Look, Ames . . ." My feelings were complicated. On the one hand, Amy goes too far. I mean, she'd walk a marathon *barefoot* across a desert in support of Rights for Nomad Women. On the other hand, if *nobody* ever went whole hog, I guess nothing would ever improve, so in a way I admire her for sticking out her neck. What I said to her at this point was, "The best thing about winning this money is that we can each do what we want . . ."

"Except that for you, having it all is going to mean three blondes on a surfboard. *California!*" she moaned, as if it were a disease. "Okay, I won't argue with you now," she went on, "but I hope I can get you to change your mind. Can you come down to Murray next weekend? I'd like you to meet some people."

"Okay, sure."

She smiled and her tone of disgust faded. "Sorry for nagging you, but—I can't help it, Mike. There's so much that's *bad* in the world—"

I nodded. "As soon as I get my money, I'll send you a check."

"Thanks, but there's more than money involved. I want you to understand what I'm doing."

I saw that her eyes were filling with tears—that's what happens when Amy gets wound up. "Hey, we're millionaires!" I reminded her. "This is no time to bawl! I'll come down to Murray. Can't you miss classes, by the way, to come to Trenton with us tomorrow?"

"I have an exam."

"Oh, well—okay." Even two and a half million bucks landing on our heads wasn't enough to get Amy to take a day off.

My parents finally left to take Amy to school, and Grandma left with them.

"Want to come with us to Amy's school?" my dad asked Grandma.

"No, no, I got to get home," she said. "I got to turn on the TV."

"Don't raise the roof too high while we're gone," my mom warned me.

"Why don't you put the lottery ticket in my desk drawer for safekeeping," my dad suggested.

Amy gave me a sincere hug. "See you next weekend, then. Good-bye, Richie Rich."

After they'd left, I stood by the window, trying to get used to my new position. How much should I give to Amy? What should I buy my grandma, an ermine or a mink? What would Sheila say, and people at school? How would Barry react when I told him? Out of all my friends, he was the one I was the most anxious to impress.

I picked up a pencil and began doodling dollar signs and then long rows of moneybags, but I hadn't been alone for more than a few minutes when I saw Barry's Buick pull up. There they were, getting out of the car, shortest to tallest: Ronnie, gremlinlike, followed by massive Lingo, then blond, frizzy-haired Barry, looking suave in a long leather coat. I opened the door before they rang the bell, patting Muttsy to calm her nervousness, so she wouldn't think the guys were dognappers on the attack. "Hi, come on in."

"Forget the small talk." Barry brushed by me. "Where's the TV? I'm in the middle of watching something."

"It's on the sunporch," I said as he whizzed through the hall. I caught Ronnie's eye. "You didn't say anything?"

He shook his head. "No offense, but they didn't want to come. I had to tell Barry that you have the money you owe him, and I told Lingo you've got a case of beer. So how does it feel?" he asked under his breath.

"Fantastic!"

Meanwhile Lingo had gone into the living room, where he was staring the way he always does in my house. "You *sure* you're Italian, Bronti? Where's the plastic seat covers and big gold lamps like we got at my place?"

"I'm only half Italian," I told him. "My mom's German and Irish. Plus my parents are into being low-key."

"*No*-key, I'd call it." Lingo shook his head in disbelief. "You don't even have a TV in your living room? What do you *do* when you're in here?"

"We sit around talking about how people like you have gone softheaded from watching the box. Come out on the porch, man, before you start suffering from TV deprivation." I steered all two hundred pounds of him out of the living room. "Sit down," I said, "I've got something major to tell you guys."

"Where's the beer first, Mike?" Lingo asked. "Ron said you had beer."

"Just a *minute*." Man, the *rudeness*. "Barry"—I kicked his fancy leather boots—"how about it? Don't you think for one second you could bag the TV?" I stared impatiently until they both looked at me. "I asked Ron to bring you over here special. I just found out I won two and a half million in the lottery today."

"So did my mother," Barry said.

Lingo's forehead furrowed. "What was that, Mike?"

"I won over two million dollars!"

Lingo looked at me mournfully. "Quit goofing on us, Bronti. Ronnie said you had beer. Was that a put-on, too?"

"Some friends you guys are!" I pulled the ticket out of my pocket. "Here, look at this!"

"You're a lousy actor, Bronti." Barry motioned for me to move out of his way. "I've got to switch channels. I need to check this score . . ."

I still can't believe the timing. Barry flipped the TV dial. "Go back to thirty!" I shouted, turning it myself. There on 30, at that exact moment, was my family. My grandma was wiping lipstick off my cheek. "See?" I pointed, gloating. "What did I tell you, *see?*"

Barry stared. Lingo's chin dropped as they watched my grandma waving hello to her friends.

"It's real, now, isn't it? Nothing's real till you see it on TV, right? Apologize!" I demanded, grabbing them both by the neck.

Ronnie was standing with his arms folded, smiling and tweaking this little mustache of his, and the other two were twisting out of my grip. As soon as the interview ended, all three of them pounced on me, lifting me up on their shoulders and then tossing me, full-force, down on the couch.

"So, Bronti"—Barry brushed himself off when the free-for-all was over—"two and a half million. What'll that come to, about a hundred thou a year for twenty years?"

"I guess so." Was that how they paid it? I'd been thinking all along it would come in one lump sum.

"Too bad Uncle Sam will keep taking half of it."

That much? "Yeah," I said calmly. Half? What a ripoff. "Still"—I shrugged—"it's a nice little sum."

"Fifty thousand a year after taxes—not too bad," Barry said, nodding. "I expect to be making that pretty soon myself."

"No kidding?" Lingo said. "Just from running errands for what's-his-name?"

"Selling townhouses!" Barry snapped. "For the Sean Burgess Company!"

Barry, who dropped out of high school a year ago, is set on proving he can out-succeed the rest of us. He started off by passing an equivalency test, which shows that he's not a dunce. Then he got hired by this Burgess guy, and he claims he's making good money. Of course, I couldn't help enjoying my new position of being one up on Barry.

"Smartest move I made in my life," Barry was saying now, "hooking up with Sean Burgess. Come by when you get that check, Bronti—I'd love you to see what Sean is selling."

That's what I mean about Barry, about my wanting to impress him. Here I'd just won a once-in-a-lifetime lottery and we were talking about *him*. Ronnie must have been reading my mind, because he turned from Barry to me. "Mike," he said pointedly, "let's see the lottery ticket."

I passed it around, and just about then, as my dad had predicted, the phone started to ring. One call after another, from people who'd seen *The Mike Bronti Show*—

friends, strangers, men, women. "If you're making a request to the fund," I told them, "write to this address." Whenever somebody our age called, the guys would yell into the phone, "Come on over, there's a party!" So I decided, what the heck, we were here and my parents were away, why not celebrate? I got in touch with a few people myself and told them to spread the word around. I tried to reach Sheila, but she still didn't answer. Meanwhile the guys went down to our basement and found some beer, and the celebration began.

Well, the party sort of mushroomed. How could I say yes to some and no to others? Naturally the kids I had invited brought along friends. Most of them also brought their own beer and stereo tapes. The house got so noisy I couldn't hear the phone anymore, but Ron sat by it patiently, playing his fake-answering-machine game.

"The number you have reached," I heard him saying, "is that of New Jersey's youngest lottery winner. If you want to meet the solid-gold kid in person, come to the party in progress now . . ."

And they did, from all over, including kids I barely knew—Lingo's wrestling team, three dudes who came on motorcycles, a girl named Mandy with pink hair. At the peak I'd say there were fifty kids circulating around the downstairs, with another half dozen lost in far corners of the house. "Don't raise the roof while we're gone!" my mom had said. I was glad she wasn't there to see us. Basically, I got some good cartoon material: Lottery winner handing beers all around. Swarms of women kissing him in exchange for a look at the ticket. Muttsy diving under the couch at the sight of the motorcycle dudes. The wrestling team pinning me and pretending to swipe the ticket. This friend of mine from work, Daryl Mabry, breakdancing and busting a leg off the coffee table.

"What's this fund you're starting?" everyone kept asking. "Is it for anybody, or just for orphans and like that?"

"People who need something," I stalled. To tell the truth, I wasn't sure.

"How about if I ask for a nose job?" a girl wanted to know. "My nose is, like, you know, a handicap."

"Yeah, well, write me a letter," I told her. I couldn't make major decisions at this point, I was too busy being the host. Certain women needed my attention. I thought guiltily of Sheila again, but how could I phone her with so many calls coming in? In addition, there were several problems, so that people kept needing my advice: What to do about the spilled beer and about Muttsy refusing to come out from under the couch. Ordinarily I would have been annoyed at the clods who were careless, or panicked at the thought of facing my parents, but in the golden glow of my win, everything seemed cool. Beer spilled? Open another one. Muttsy shy? Let her have her privacy. Even when the neighbors came over and threatened to call the cops, I took it in my stride.

I was just showing my neighbors the lottery ticket and asking the kids who were dancing to lower the sound a little when Ronnie called me to the telephone. "Take this one live," he said.

" 'Lo?"

"Mike, I been trying to get through!"

"Oh, hi, Grandma. The phone's been ringing. Did you see us on TV?"

"We looked *beautiful*! But listen, Daddy and Mom aren't home yet?"

"No."

"Are the doors locked?"

I cupped my hand over the bottom of the receiver. "Why?"

"You got to be careful now that you got this money. I was talking to Margaret—somebody could steal the ticket or *worse*, you know what I mean?"

"Don't worry, Grandma. I've got friends with me."

"Friends? Who?"

I paused. "One of them wrestles heavyweight. He'll protect me no matter what."

"You sure you can trust this guy?"

"Yeah, Grandma—Lingo, Joe Linganelli. He's Italian. I gave him one of your cutlets before. He said it was the best he ever ate."

"He's Italian? Okay. But don't let no strangers in."

Gleep.

"What's that noise, you still watching the TV?"

"Yeah! I'll call you tomorrow morning, Grandma. You're coming down to Trenton to pick up the check with us, right?"

"Yeah."

"Okay, see you then."

"Make your friend stay until Daddy comes back. I'd feel safer, you know? Tell him three pounds of cutlets just for him if he stays."

"Okay! Bye!"

By the time I got off the phone, luckily the party had started to break up, so I didn't have to worry about the neighbors actually calling the cops. I stood at the door as the kids left, accepting more congratulations. Barry bugged me a little by shaking hands with everyone, as if *he* were the host. Lingo was at the door with me, arms folded like a polite bouncer. It was almost as if he could read my grandma's mind. Ronnie, meanwhile, even before everyone went, had started emptying ashtrays. "Get off your duffs, you guys," he said when the four of us were alone at last. "This place is a disaster area."

"Hire a cleaning service," Barry said.

In my mellow mood that sounded like a pretty good idea, until Ronnie reminded me that my parents were due home soon.

"Come on!" Ron jabbed Lingo and Barry, and they started to help us, Lingo moving furniture back into place and Barry straightening the pictures on the walls.

It was at that point that it suddenly occurred to me that I hadn't seen the lottery ticket in a while. I stuck my hand in my pocket, but—holy hell, it wasn't there. "Who's got the ticket?" I asked casually.

The three of them stopped what they were doing and looked at me like the Three Stooges. "You were showing it to that girl with the big boobs out on the porch," Ron said.

"Check your pockets again," Barry called as I went to the porch to look.

No luck, not in my pockets, or on the porch, or under the furniture. Ron, Lingo, and I got down on our hands and knees and searched all over the floor. I heard Barry back in the living room, opening my dad's desk drawers. "Find it yet?" Lingo kept asking. "No, idiot!" I shouted. "Quit asking dumb questions!"

Now I really began to sweat. I pawed through the carton of empty beer cans. Lingo was lifting the whole couch up and Ronnie was looking under the rug. I thought of my grandma's warning that had sounded so silly. I had laughed at her for worrying, and now the ticket was gone.

"Look, it's okay," Ron said, seeing how jumpy I was. "You signed it, at least, didn't you?"

"Signed it?"

Barry stuck his head in the doorway. "You didn't *sign* it? Bronti, you nerd!"

He was smiling. I swear he was smiling. Deep down he was happy I'd lost the ticket! If I found it, I swore I'd never speak to the guy again.

"We'll find it," Ron insisted. "Did you go upstairs? Did you leave this room?"

"No, but I'll look anyway." I ran up there, and after a futile search I came running back. By now we were all basket cases. Even Barry was glassy-eyed. "Call the police," he suggested.

"And say what, that they should go out and question everybody who was here?"

"Maybe," Barry said. "Did you see the shifty eyes on those motorcycle guys?"

I got so depressed at that point—now I *was* panicked about facing my parents—that I threw myself down on my stomach, the full length of the sunporch couch. I was lying there, limp as a dead man, face buried, feet dangling, when all of a sudden Ronnie hollered.

"Hey! Hold still—here it is, here it is!"

I rolled over. *"Where?"*

Twisting my ankle and holding my foot, Ron peeled the lottery ticket off the sole of my sneaker.

"Is it okay?" I gasped. "Is it torn?"

"It's okay." He took a pen from his pocket. *"Sign* it, you fool!"

42

I did, very carefully. Then, without taking any more chances, I immediately put the ticket in my dad's desk drawer. Back on the porch, I felt like a new man. It was as if I'd won the money all over again. I even forgave Lingo's dumb questions and Barry's smile when the ticket was gone. I picked up Ron off the floor—I outweigh him enough to do that—then I put him down again and slapped palms. "Name your reward, man. How much do you want?"

"Nothing now," he said, bowing like a servant. "All I want is a partnership in New Disneyland Park."

"You got it. Hey, quick, let's finish the cleanup. My parents could be here any minute." The furniture needed straightening again after the search for the ticket. We ran around like madmen, picking up all the remaining junk. Lingo took garbage out, Ron fixed the table leg, and I sprayed Kleenair deodorizer wherever beer had been spilled.

And not a moment too soon. We had just stuffed the vacuum back in the closet and the guys were saying good night to me when my parents came home.

My mom and dad were pretty tired, but they were still hopping with excitement. "Were we on TV yet?" "Did you get many calls?" They walked into the living room.

"You vacuumed?" my mom asked. "That's nice."

My dad seemed to be sniffing the air, and I expected the third degree again, but all he asked was, "The ticket's safe?"

"Yeah," I said, exhausted but smiling. "Everything's just *fine*."

# 6

"So"—my dad sat back after we'd taken the phone off the hook and eaten some of my mom's cold roast—"what are you going to do, now that you're the first Bronti millionaire?"

"Go to Cummings Institute of Art in California."

"California." My mom's teacup clattered. "Amy's talking about Africa, and you're thinking of California. Aren't the best art schools near here? Why go so far?"

"The best schools for *fine* arts are here," I agreed, "but Cummings is good for commercial art. Plus, it's close to the film industry, Disney Studios and all that."

My mom shook her head. "Aren't we lucky," she said to my dad. "Mike wins a fortune, goes off to California, and sends Amy around the world. And we don't see either one of them anymore. That's really some luck."

"Come on," I said, "neither one of us is going away forever. Aren't you glad we have all these possibilities?"

"I guess so," she admitted. "I just don't want everything to change too fast."

"The big thing," my dad said, "is don't make any rash

decisions. See my accountant, Phil Mercer, this week. Meanwhile, collect the check tomorrow and put it in the bank."

"I'm keeping out *something*!"

"Well, some spending money, sure, but he says you'd be foolish jumping into anything too quick. Now, what if you don't get into this California school? Will you be satisfied to go to Murray? Maybe you should start looking for a good business school. This income is nice, of course, but it's not forever. After twenty years it runs out."

"Why worry about twenty years from now? Besides, I'll get into Cummings," I said confidently. I was feeling unbeatable, I swear.

"And how about your job?" my dad asked. "Your job down at Beefarama?"

I made a gross noise. "The best thing about winning the lottery will be telling Nevelson I quit. How about you two?" I said. "Wouldn't you like some time off?"

"I couldn't, Mike," my mom said. "I couldn't desert my second graders. Even my taking off *one day* to go down to Trenton with you tomorrow will make them upset."

"Dad?" I asked. "How about you?"

He stared at a speck on the wall. "I'm going to Trenton tomorrow, sure."

"I mean after that. Switch jobs," I suggested.

"Are you kidding? I can't do that."

"I thought things weren't going too well," I began.

"Who said so?"

"I thought *you* did. With this money I'm getting, you could quit and do something else."

He looked at me impatiently. "It's *your* money."

"It's for all of us!"

"Like I said, it's a nice sum," my dad went on as if he hadn't heard me. "You can pay for your own education. That'll give Mom and me a break. I'd like to see you studying business, but who am I to say? Take art. Major in drawing Mickey Mouse—study whatever you want to. I just hope you'll invest the bulk of the money in something safe, so you'll be secure for life."

My mom got up. "It's getting late. We have years ahead to talk about this. I don't know about you two, but I'm going to bed."

"I'll be up soon." My dad rose and wandered off to the living room.

I got up too. "What a day, huh?" I said to my mom. "I'd better let Muttsy out."

"Lock the door when you bring her in," she called from the stairs. "And Mike, please put the receiver back on the hook for the night."

No sooner had I hung up the phone than it rang, and I picked it up in the kitchen. "Hello?"

"Mike!"

"Sheila!"

"*Mike!*" she repeated. "I've been trying to call you for two hours and your phone's always busy. Mike, it's unbelievable! I've been trying to call *since I heard!*"

Oh, man, this was the perfect end to a perfect day. I pictured her sitting on her bed, which I'd never seen, except in my imagination. She'd be surrounded by stuffed animals, probably, wearing a frilly nightgown, her lips pressed close to the telephone. I grinned. "How'd you find out?"

"I was down at my cousin's since this morning, and when I got off the bus, coming back, I saw this girl from school, Mandy—"

"Pink hair?"

"Yeah, Mandy Calise. She told me."

"Mandy Calise, sure, sure. Listen, I tried to call you all day."

"Mike, two million? I can't believe it! Mandy said you had a party."

"Yeah, on the spur of the moment. You were the first person I called, but nobody answered your phone."

"I'm *dying* that I was out! Of all days to be away! Mike, what's the exact amount?"

"Two point four million."

"*Eeeeee!* What are you going to *do* with it?"

I pictured her full, rosy lips saying "dooo." "I'm pretty flexible," I told her. "Have any ideas?"

"You'll get a car, I hope. Something sporty, but also really comfortable. You know that car Bob Hammond has? That's what I like. What else are you going to get? What did your parents say? How was the party? Who was there? I'm so mad I missed it! I should have told you where I was going!"

"You were mad at me, remember? We were having a fight. Are you ready to forgive me now?" I kidded her.

"Yes, I'm *sorry*. No more fights!"

While she was saying how great the news was, how I could quit my job and spend more time with her now, I had a big urge to run over to her house and join her there on the bed. This was just wishing, of course. Her parents never left us alone. I had once drawn a cartoon of her father locking her into a suit of armor and throwing the key away. Up until this point she'd always done exactly what her parents wanted her to. Was there a chance of making a chink in the armor now? I couldn't help wondering.

"Was Lynne at your party?" Sheila asked, jolting me out of my fantasy.

"No! Just kids from school," I assured her, "—whoever happened to hear." Sheila's jealous, let's face it. Usually I don't mind that much, but when she accuses me of being interested in Lynne Carter, I'm annoyed. Lynne's just a good friend.

"Mike," Sheila said now, "I know I shouldn't be worrying at a time like this, but—oh, no, I'm afraid to ask!"

"What?"

"What does this mean about—about your going away?"

That's been another problem between us. Sheila keeps hoping I'll forget about Cummings. She's planning to stick around, go to Glenfield Community. "Well, California's more possible now," I told her.

Silence.

But this was no time for an argument. "Of course, I haven't gotten accepted yet," I said, to soften the blow. "But if I do, you'll be glad, you'll see. You'll fly out to visit me. I'll come home for vacations. Anything's possible."

"Maybe—"

"Yeah?"

"Maybe you'll change your mind, once your money comes."

I knew I wouldn't, but I didn't want to tell her that, not at this particular moment. Why upset her? This was the happiest day of my life, and I wanted it to be happy for her, too. "Listen, don't worry," I begged her. "Just concentrate on how we'll celebrate."

"How?"

"We'll go wherever you want."

"Really? I can't wait! Mike?" Her voice dropped an octave now. "My mom's knocking on my door. She wants me to get off the phone."

"Should I come over instead?"

"Mike! You're so bad! I've got to hang up. I'm sorry."

"Not as sorry as I am. Let me come over, okay? You could let me in after your parents go to—"

"You're crazy! Mike. Oh!" Her voice rose again. "I completely forgot to tell you. I was at my cousin's today, Sunny's? Guess what, she and Billy got engaged!"

"No kidding. Big day for them, too. Sheila, just for a couple of minutes?" I tried again. "I could climb in your window—"

"No! My mom's *listening*," she whispered. "I'll see you in school!"

"Not tomorrow. I'm going to Trenton. I'll call you when I get back—"

"Good night, Mike," she murmured hurriedly. "Sweet dreams!" She hung up.

I sat for a second by the phone, thinking of how Sheila must look as she crawled into bed. Hair tumbling to her shoulders, skin smelling of lemon soap. I could take her with me to California. . . . Then Muttsy started barking and I remembered I still had to let her out.

When I opened the front door, Muttsy immediately ran to the curb, and I noticed a car parked there with somebody sitting in it. I tried to see who it was, but the street light wasn't bright enough. Then Muttsy barked again and the car *vroomed* and took off.

I brought Mutts back in, locked the door, and turned off the lights in the house so that I stood in the hallway, completely in the dark. *Unbelievable*, I thought. *Me. This has happened to me.* I couldn't resist looking at the ticket one more time before I went to bed.

I felt my way into the living room, with Muttsy panting

behind me. The mirror over the mantel reflected lights from outside. Weird. I groped for the switch, but I couldn't find it. Muttsy growled at me warningly. I thought of what my grandma had said earlier and of the car I'd just seen: LOTTERY TICKET STOLEN, I thought. TEEN WINNER AXED TO DEATH IN OWN HOUSE.

I inched toward my dad's desk. I had to check on that ticket. Reaching out, I touched flesh—somebody was there, stealing it! "Hey!"

The light went on and who did I see sitting there? "Dad! What are you *doing*?"

"Thinking," he said calmly. "Mulling things over."

"Why didn't you *say* something? Holy cannoli! I thought somebody had broken in!"

"I didn't hear you." He swiveled around. "Don't worry—the ticket's safe. I decided to lock the drawer, and I was just sitting here . . . Mike?"

"Yeah?"

"I've been thinking. This could make all the difference in your life, you know. . . ." He got up, and for a second he looked as if he was going to put his arms around me or something. He backed off, though. "It's not that money guarantees happiness," he said, embarrassed. "But damn it, it helps." He paused. "What do you say? Let's go get some sleep." On the way up he turned to me. "Mike?"

"Yeah?"

"I'm happy for you, really happy for you."

"Thanks." I smiled. "Good night!"

Sometimes it's a drag when you can't sleep, but that night it didn't matter. My head was so full of great ideas that I was glad to be awake. I considered getting up to draw something about a kid who wins a lottery. Nah, I thought, the best humor is closest to reality. The idea was too farfetched!

The next morning I woke up early. No sense wasting time sleeping. I kept calling the lottery commission, and they finally answered at nine o'clock. They wanted me and my parents down at the State House for a press conference in two hours. Hunting for something to wear, I ran around pulling out bureau drawers. Because of all the confusion the day before, my clothes were still in the washing machine, wet. What to wear? In comic strips they always show guys dressed in a barrel. How about going to the press conference wearing just the winning ticket, like a fig leaf?

I didn't have to go quite that far. I found a decent pair of pants and a sweater, and I got dressed, somewhere between answering all the telephone calls. The school phoned to check on my absence, and I had the pleasure of

51

giving the reason: I just happened to be going down to Trenton to claim over two million dollars! Some more calls came in to the fund, including one from a man who was blind, who hoped I'd be able to get him a seeing-eye dog.

Eventually my parents and I got ourselves together and went to pick up Grandma. "Where's this we're going?" she asked.

"To the State House, where the governor is."

"I hope he's home," she said, showing me the plastic bag hanging over her arm. "I brought cake and a bottle of wine. It wouldn't be right going there empty-handed."

As it turned out, the governor was busy running the State of New Jersey. The lottery commissioner met us, though, and the treasurer of the state, and my grandma gave the goodies to them. They ushered us into a wood-paneled room, very fancy, with velvet drapes and a big conference table. Aides were running around, like Huey, Dewey, and Louie, verifying my ticket and certifying my I.D. Then the photographers positioned themselves, ready to shoot, and the treasurer handed me my check for $94,190. Flashbulbs went off—*aiiiieeeeeee!*

"That's the first of twenty installments," the commissioner explained to me. "You'll get approximately that amount on or about this date for nineteen more years. Twenty percent for federal income tax has already been taken out, but you'll probably have to pay additional taxes . . ."

I tried to listen, but I was too dazed. Meanwhile reporters crowded around me, some from newspapers, some from TV and radio stations. More flashbulbs popped and the reporters kept firing away. One of the questions they asked me was "Can you see any special problems, winning this easy money at your age?"

"Problems? What, me worry? If there are any, I'm willing to risk them," I said.

On the way to the car with my family, though, after the conference was over, I had a delayed reaction to the reporter. "Easy money! The odds on winning are *one in two million*. How could any money be *un*easier to get!"

"Easy money," my grandma said with a chuckle, and even though it wasn't that funny, we laughed, as they say, all the way to the bank.

Have you ever had a thousand bucks cash in your pocket? Wait—I'm getting ahead of myself. We stopped for a big lunch to celebrate, and then my parents said they'd take me to the Glenfield State Bank. That reminded me of being a little kid, being taken to deposit my birthday money, so I convinced them to drop me off. I wanted to go by myself.

"Don't talk to nobody on the way in," my grandma warned when I got out of the car.

"Just put the whole thing into a high-interest savings account until you see Mercer," my dad called.

"Okay, thanks for the ride," I said, "and don't wait for me for dinner. I'm going over to Beefarama, and then I'm probably going out."

I had always thought of banks as boring places. And from the cold, glassy look of this one I wasn't about to change my mind. Going through the revolving door, I wished that Ron was here with me. He would know how to stare down that guard who was giving me the fish-eye.

"Need some help, sir?" the guard asked.

Yeah, hand over all you've got, I felt like saying, just to shake things up in this echoing morgue. "Uh, yes," I said almost meekly instead. "I've got a lottery check to deposit."

"Lottery check?" Suddenly I had a friend at Glenfield State. The guard told a teller, and the teller read my letter of identification and spread the word to employees and customers about who I was. Next thing I knew, the branch manager welcomed me personally and started mumbling about things to invest in, but I told him all I wanted was a checking account.

"Checking?" He seemed surprised.

"Yes," I said. "You pay interest on it, don't you?"

"Yes."

A checking account, wasn't that what my dad had said? I filled out the papers they put in front of me, and they gave me a checkbook with some temporary checks. "How do I get some cash?" I asked.

"We ordinarily have to wait until the check you deposit clears," the teller said, "but in this case we can make an exception. How much cash would you like?"

"A thousand—make it ten one-hundred-dollar bills, please."

She counted out new hundreds, with Ben Franklin on them. "A penny saved is a penny earned," the guy had said. What would old Ben have thought of lotteries? I wondered. Something I didn't realize until that minute was that the bank had a special deal on. They gave you a gift for every five thousand you put in an account. I did some quick figuring. "Eighteen gifts!" I pointed to a clock radio, a Walkman, a toaster, and some other appliances, which they said they would deliver, at some point, to my house.

I was flying high as I shook the hand of the manager and left Glenfield State. Ten one-hundreds, plus a checkbook in my pocket, showing a balance of $93,190. Some switcheroo from the poor-boy me of yesterday morning depressed about owing Barry DeVane thirty bucks.

I felt like *showing* somebody right away, but school wasn't out yet. Walking down Main Street with my pockets bulging, I figured I'd drop in at Freddy's News. The shops on the way there—man, the shops! I'd lived in Glenfield my whole life and never noticed that right here in town you could buy diamonds and furs. And *cars*, of course, at Stenton Motors. I could stop right this minute if I wanted to and buy a—what? A sports car? A van? I was tempted but also impatient, so I went on to Freddy's, bouncing with every step.

From a block away you can smell Freddy's, and the smell gets stronger and stronger—a sweet combination of comic books, Coke syrup, cigars, and bubble gum. On the rack outside the store I saw that the *Glenfield Independent* had a story on the front page about me: LOCAL TEENAGER WINS N. J. LOTTERY PRIZE. I read it quickly, happy to see that they only misspelled my name twice. I tucked a couple of copies under my arm and went inside. "Hi, Freddy."

"My winner!" He came out from behind the counter and threw his arms around me like a long-lost son. I'm not sure exactly what Freddy's story is, but he's had a rough life. He has no kids, only his nephew, Martin, who works in the store with him. Anyway, both of them were so happy, and not just because they were getting a bonus for selling me the winning ticket.

"Bronti!" "Hey, dude!" "Congratulations!"

Amazing—I was surrounded by guys I hardly knew, who happened to be hanging out. I couldn't have asked for a better audience. They crowded around me, and pounded

55

me, and went nuts when I showed them my ten wallet pictures of Ben Franklin.

One guy moved up from behind the others. "Remember me?"

"Hey, you're Lennie Thompson, aren't you?" He was the guy who had called me, the one who had bought a ticket when I did—a tall skinny kid with a huge Adam's apple. "If it weren't for you," I told him, "I might not be standing here now!" I shook his hand. "Freddy," I called, "lottery tickets all around—and cigarettes or whatever." I threw one of my hundreds on the counter. "Treat Thompson right!" What a kick, to be peeling off bills in that place where I'd won them, breathing in that candy store smell that was the sweetest in the world.

While I was helping the guys pick their numbers and buying myself a few tickets, the door opened and who should come in but Barry DeVane. "Hey, man," I said, "great timing. How come you're not working?"

"I am. Sean—my boss—sent me over to get a paper. We've got an ad in today. Did you get your check already?"

"Yeah, and I've been to the bank." I got a kick out of spreading my wallet open and thumbing through my hundreds. I handed him one and said, "Time to settle up debts."

He looked at me. "Thanks, but I don't have change on me."

"It doesn't matter," I told him. "Go on, keep the change."

"Thanks."

"What'd you owe him?" the guys wanted to know.

"Thirty," I said. I *loved* this.

"Only thirty? And you gave him a hundred? Bronti's *all right*!"

"Where are you heading now?" Barry asked me, as if he was annoyed with the attention I was getting.

"I have to go over to Beefarama and tell my boss I'm going to retire."

"Want a ride?" Barry offered.

"Sure, I'd appreciate it. So long, you guys!"

"Got a big enough mattress to hide that money in?" Freddy called after me. Lennie Thompson started to follow me out, but then he changed his mind and stayed back.

"See you!" Inhaling one last lungful of Freddy's News perfume, I went outside with Barry and we walked to his car.

On the way Barry opened his newspaper and folded the page back. "Get a load of this, man, the Burgess Company ad." BUY THE TOWNHOUSE OF YOUR DREAMS. LUXURIOUS EXTRAS. DISCOUNTED PRICES. "If I had the capital you have, I'd invest in a couple of these so fast."

He unlocked the car and I got in. "A couple?" I said. "What would I do with even *one*?"

"Resell at a profit or live in it yourself!"

"I *have* a place to live."

"With your parents? Now that you're a millionaire?"

"Yeah, but—" I paused. "I won't even be around here. I'll probably be going to California to school."

Barry started up the motor. "*Look*, I'm not going to try to talk you out of school, man. You'll see for yourself how unnecessary it is, once you start getting used to having money. If I were you, I'd bag high school. What do you need five more months of *that* for? See this?" He rattled the paper as he steered with one hand toward Main Street. "Special deals now, arranged by the Burgess Company—"

"Nice." I yawned.

"Country living, one-half hour from downtown Glenfield. Tennis courts, pool, sauna . . ." he went on. "Think of the women you could entertain if you owned one of these."

"Come on, Barry. I've *got* a woman. Anyway, why would I want a place there?"

"What *are* you going to invest in," he smirked, stopping for a red light, "ninety-four thousand dollars' worth of old comic books?"

"Maybe. Old ones are valuable. I'd rather put money into them than *townhouses.*"

"Listen"—Barry looked at me impatiently as he started up again—"I'm the only friend you've got with his head in the real world. Seriously, watch yourself. You're not going to get involved with some kind of harebrained scheme with *Ronnie,* are you? Ron's got a great imagination, but if we're talking business, the guy is straight from outer space." He wove his way through the traffic now and cleared his throat loudly. "If you're not interested in a townhouse for yourself, how about lending me enough to buy one?"

"How much do they go for?" I asked.

"They start at $150,000. You could lend me enough for a down payment, maybe. What's the matter, don't you trust me?"

"Hey, Beefarama's coming up," I said. "Better stop here—right here."

Barry came to a screeching halt. "Don't you trust me?" he repeated. "What about all the times you've owed *me* money?"

I opened the door and got out. "Thirty bucks isn't exactly the same as thirty grand or whatever."

"Smartest move you could make would be lending me thirty grand," he called after me. "I'd be paying you big interest!"

Cars were honking behind him now. "Glad you have my interest in mind!" I yelled. "Thanks for the ride. I'm going to take you guys out on the town soon." I felt good as I waved and headed toward Beefarama. Barry *must* be impressed with me, if he was asking me to lend him thirty grand.

8

There in front of me, at the sign of the big red *B*, was Glenfield Beefarama, where I had been putting my life in jeopardy by working fifteen hours most weeks. The risks were sliced fingertips, toxic pickle fumes, and terminal acne from grease particles. On the plus side, though, were all the cartoons inspired by my working in the place. (In frame one a customer asks, "Waiter, is there any creamy Italian dressing on the menu?" In frame two the waiter is madly wiping with a napkin. "Excuse me, ma'am, there was, but I got it all off!")

What was happening in there? As soon as I went in the employees' entrance, I heard lots of voices out in front. Monday is usually the deadest, but today Nevelson himself was behind the grill. Usually Nevelson is too much of a hotshot to do any menial labor, so I knew something very unusual must be going on. I stood there watching him for a second, thinking how much he looks like Dick Tracy—I've drawn him often, in strips that I show to my friend Lynne, called "The Adventures of Ptomaine Tom."

"You're going to tell me you're quitting, aren't you?" he spat out, without looking at me.

"Yeah, well, I won this—"

"I know."

No congratulations or anything. All he said was "I know."

"I got ten nine-year-olds out there," he moaned, "plus the Glenfield Golden Agers. Meanwhile Mabry called in sick, and now you're going to tell me *why should you work when you can buy up the chain?*"

For a split second I had a fantasy of me owning the place, but then I inhaled the smell of grease again and my fantasy burned out. "I could help you for an hour or so," I said, looking around to see where Lynne was.

"An hour." He looked disgusted. "Okay, what are you waiting for? Get into the suit!"

I choked. "The suit?" He was referring to the Beefarama Bunny suit, complete with a huge papier-mâché head and stand-up ears, that one of us sometimes wears when there's a large party of kids.

Nevelson glared at me. "Yeah, the *suit,* and speed it up!"

I shuffled to the employees' room, cursing myself for getting into this. But the thought of sticking Lynne with all those people made me grit my teeth and pull off my shirt. Next I took off my pants and stepped into the fuzzy white costume. Zipping up the back as well as I could, I glanced at myself in the full-length mirror. My cottontail was drooping pathetically, hanging by a thread. There were catsup stains on my forepaws. Who would think, to look at me now, that I was a teenage millionaire? With the rabbit head in my hands, I came out of the employees' room and ran smack into Lynne.

She threw her arms around me, crushing the rabbit whiskers. "I *heard*, Mike, congratulations!"

"Thanks."

She patted my furry paws. "You're working today anyway?"

"Just for an hour, to help out Nevelson." To help out *her*, was the truth of it. "Unbelievable news, huh?"

"I'm so happy for you, I can't tell you." She straightened the whiskers on the rabbit head. "What will you do with the money?"

I noticed Nevelson approaching. "Start a rest home for ex-Beefarama employees," I said. "Come on, we're getting the evil eye. We'll talk after the rush."

Lynne helped me put on the rabbit head. The air was terrible inside. Then we both went out front, where kids were winging placemats like Frisbees and the Golden Agers were asking if we had low-cal French fries. It was rough, coming off Cloud 9 and pretending to be a bunny, but I tried hard, saying "What's up, Doc?" and tossing the placemats back at the kids.

I don't want to remember that next half hour or so. The mother in charge of the kids was impatient. "I hope we won't have to wait," she said. "They're *children*, you know." It's good she told me. I thought they were orangutans, the way they grabbed at me as if my ears were bananas. "We want Whammo-shakes!" they started chanting, meanwhile making fun of my droopy tail. I wrote down the kids' orders while Lynne waited on the Golden Agers, who were impatient for a different reason—they wanted to get home before dusk.

When we took the orders into the kitchen, Nevelson was cursing and banging the grill with a pan. It wasn't heating right. "Ha!" he snorted. "We claim we're in the fast food business—what a laugh!" Lynne and I began serving hot tea and Whammo-shakes while Nevelson kept banging and fiddling. Finally he got the grill working, but not before the customers staged a revolt. The kids didn't complain at first—they were too busy smashing empty paper cups and blowing straw wrappers at each other. It was the seniors who were stamping and muttering "What service!" "Not like it used to be years ago!"

I drew a few caricatures to distract the adults and told the kids some stupid rabbit jokes, and then, just as the kids began to yell "We want food!" Nevelson gave us a sign that the orders were ready. He helped us serve, which was nice. The kids tore into their burgers, and the Golden Agers nibbled at theirs, while I prepared to bring on dessert. When the tables were all cleared and I put down the ice cream cake in front of the birthday boy, I noticed the seniors eyeing it and I got an idea. Lynne and Nevelson were in the kitchen. I went back to the freezer and brought an identical cake to the seniors. "This is on the house," I said.

"What's that?"

"Say *what*?"

At first they didn't believe me, but I assured them I wasn't kidding. "Because you had to wait so long," I explained, and then I decided, what the hell . . . "Mr. Nevelson, the manager, doesn't want you to pay at all. The whole meal's on the house. We're really sorry you had to wait." You should have seen their faces—I don't know if any of them were poor or not. Maybe they weren't, but so what? Getting a free meal really made their day. I thought of telling them it was on me because of my lottery win, but then, as Lynne came back, I decided I wouldn't. Instead, I whispered to Lynne. "I told them their dinner's free because we kept them waiting. Give me the bill, but don't tell them I'm paying."

"Mike, you're amazing. How did you learn so fast how to be rich?"

When I heard Lynne's reaction, I went to the kids' table, too, and told the mother she didn't have to pay for the party. She and some of the seniors started heaping thanks on me, but I said, "No, no, don't thank *me*. If you want to show your appreciation, just tell the manager as you leave that this is the best Beefarama in the chain."

By the time both groups finished their cake, they were getting along like one big happy family. Then they all put on their coats and called to Nevelson as they left, "You got a wonderful place here!" "This is the best Beefarama!" Nevelson looked as if he'd been zapped by a stun-gun. "Thank you," he said, mystified. "Thanks, thanks a lot."

The total bill for the two groups came to ninety-some dollars, so when they'd all gone, I took off my rabbit head and put one of my hundreds in the cash register drawer.

Lynne came up behind me. "I love that you did that. It's going to be boring around here with you gone."

I knew what she meant. I would have hated for her to quit and leave me here without her. She was the one person I could say *anything* to. She gave me advice about Sheila and encouragement in my drawing. Ron was interested in drawing, of course, but most of the time we were competitors. "If it gets too boring, you can always quit," I said to Lynne.

Her eyebrows shot up. "I need the job."

She's a freshman at Wayne College, near here, and she pays a lot of her own expenses. I thought for a second.

"Hey, wait. You've just been awarded a Beefarama Scholarship—"

She smiled and shook her head.

"Why not?"

"I know what you're offering, Mike—help from you, which is nice of you, but I wouldn't. I've got this crazy old-fashioned idea that I should do things on my own. I hear you said on TV that you were starting some kind of charity. Sounds good. If you need help with it, just give me a call."

"In that case, give me your number." Until then I had never called Lynne at home. It would be the only way to talk to her now, though, so I wrote her number down. "I've got to go."

"Better change first," she said. "Otherwise you might be chased by a dog or something."

"Yeah, you're right." I slipped into the employees' room, put on my own clothes, and came out again. "I'll call you soon," I said, surprised that I had such mixed feelings about quitting.

"Don't be sad, you won the lottery!" She smiled, as if she'd been reading my mind.

I was just about to give her a good-bye hug when Ptomaine Tom came and found us.

"Here," he said, shoving an envelope in my hand.

"What's this?"

"You have that coming."

Opening it, I saw a check for all the pay he owed me, including today. Nice, Tom's not wanting to owe me anything. I cleared my throat. "Thanks."

He glanced away as he spoke. "I appreciate your helping out, Mike. A lot of employees wouldn't have even bothered calling in to quit." Then he turned to me again, sadly. "You'll probably have better things to do, but any time you want to, feel free to drop in."

I looked at him, and then at Lynne, and suddenly I felt a little choked up, so, to keep from making a fool of myself, I said good-bye and went out.

9

Because of talking to Lynne again and taking down her address, I felt a little guilty when I came out of Beefarama. Not that there was any reason for Sheila to be jealous, but the fact of the matter was, I hadn't seen Sheila since I'd won. I stopped at an outdoor phone and called her. "Hi, Sheila."

"Mike!"

"I got my check—$94,190! What's happening? How was school?"

"Okay," she said. "Everybody was talking about you!"

"Yeah? What did they say?"

"That they wish they were you. Somebody heard you're going to rent a yacht that goes around the Statue of Liberty and take the senior class on a party cruise . . ."

"Not a bad idea," I said. Then I filled her in on my day.

"I'm so glad you quit working," she said. "That's the best part of all of this."

"Yeah."

"I haven't seen you in two days," Sheila murmured. "Can you come over right now?"

"Okay, let's go out—"

"Forget it, Mike, not on a school night. My parents'll let you come here, though. My mom was asking 'When are we going to see him? He hasn't even been over since he won!'"

I wanted to see Sheila, but not in her living room with her parents. That's the way it always was when I went over to her house. Sitting around with her parents provided me with material for cartoons, but that was the most I could say about it. "I'll see you tomorrow," I said. "Eight o'clock at my locker." After I had hung up, I remembered that I was supposed to call Ronnie.

"The number you have reached, 555-1731, is that of the Schwartzes of Glenfield, a family distinguished primarily for its talented offspring, Ron. If you are calling to award a prize, a fellowship, or a grant, at the sound of the tone please—"

"This is the Bronti Fund!" I shouted. "We don't give awards to answering machines. If a *person* had picked up, he'd have gotten a half million bucks."

"Mike?" Ron sounded manic. "I hoped it was you, man. You got the check? How'd it go? How was Trenton? Where are you now?"

"Main and Hutton."

"Come on over! I've got business to discuss."

"Wait a minute, I haven't eaten yet, have you?"

"No, my parents are away. I'm an abandoned child."

"So come meet me, I'll take you out."

"Bring something *here*," he insisted, "I've got big things to *show*."

"Okay," I agreed. "Is Chinese all right?"

"You're on."

Hanging up, I went to My Lin's, Glenfield's best-known

Chinese takeout, where I ordered two of everything on the menu. So *this* was what it was like to be rich. I pulled out my wallet. Ron wanted Chinese food? He was getting a dinner he'd never forget.

I ended up needing a ride to Ron's in My Lin's delivery mobile—one of those scooters with a sidecar and a storage thing on the back. I had ordered so much stuff that it was piled around me in the sidecar. And when I told the driver I was celebrating a lottery win, he leaned on the horn all the way there.

Ron was home alone, so we had privacy for our oriental orgy. By the way, you wouldn't believe what it's like in Schwartz's house. It's a museum, full of stuff that he and his parents buy, that used to be called junk but is now called collectible—glass vases, movie posters, old gumball machines. We spread out our feast on the big round oak table in the kitchen and drank our tea out of Orphan Annie mugs. While I was pouring the hot-and-sour soup, Ron took out a bunch of drawings from a big envelope. *"These* are what I was referring to," he said.

I should explain how I met Ron. He was the new kid in fourth grade—an oddball, kind of scrawny, into science fiction like mad. The teacher, Miss Kreps, felt sorry for him because the kids called him Spaceman, so she asked me to be his friend, and in those days I used to do whatever a teacher said. It turned out we had a lot in common—cartooning, mainly. Anyway, there we were, eight years later, with Ron showing me his latest drawings over egg rolls and soup.

"I sketched the whole thing," he said, Chinese noodle crumbs in his dinky mustache.

"What whole thing?"

"The plan for our park."

I didn't tell him, but with all the excitement of the past day or two, I had practically forgotten our crazy fantasy of building an amusement park. "A park's a major thing—" I stalled. "Do you really think it's possible?"

Ron looked at me disgustedly. "What if Disney had said that?" Making room between the food cartons, he spread his drawings out.

The top of my head started to tingle, maybe from the potent mustard sauce, but I don't think so. That's the effect I often get from seeing how Ron draws. My style is simple—clean black and white, something like "Hi and Lois" or "Funky Winkerbean." Ron's style is much more witty, and original, and beautiful, and detailed.

I reached for the spicy chicken and peanuts, but my eyes were on his drawings for the park. Besides the plans, drawn to scale, there were sketches that were works of art. "I'm jealous," I admitted. "You're a goddam genius." In the past I'd felt too competitive to be able to say that, but now I could afford to be generous—I was a teenage millionaire.

"I know," he said with his usual lack of modesty. "That's what *I'm* bringing to the partnership. You're bringing the bucks."

Sipping my tea, I studied the sketches and the total conception. "When did you do all this?"

"It's been in my head for years," he said, "and then when I got home from your place Sunday night, I realized, hey, it's *possible* now. So I started to draw. Look at this"—he shoved aside the spareribs—"here's the prehistoric section." He pointed. "In honor of the capitalist behind it, we'll call the whole thing Bronti-saurus Park."

"*Arrrrgh!*" I looked at the rest of the park plans—Historyland, World of the Future. "Amazing, amazing, but where the hell would we begin?"

"By finding a site."

Ron was deep into pork and fried rice now, and I was sampling beef and bamboo shoots. "Find one where?" I asked. "There's no space like we'd need in this part of the country."

He doused his rice with soy sauce. "That's why a trip is in order. We could take it this summer—leave early to go to Cummings. You could buy a van. We'd drive across the country, looking for the right spot."

I crunched thoughtfully on a water chestnut. "A trip would be great."

Ron dipped into the lychee nuts. "We'd see real estate people, make more drawings, put a down payment on some land."

"We could hit some beaches," I added, "visit cities, meet women . . ." Sheila would kill me if she heard this— I'd be gone for months.

We kept trading more ideas as we cleaned up from dinner, and then Ron took out the fortune cookies from the bottom of the bag. He crunched his between his teeth, then pulled out his fortune and read:

" '*Help! I'm trapped in a Chinese cookie factory!*' Nah, just kidding." He squinted. " '*You have many talents.*' Bah, what else is new? Read yours."

I broke my cookie and read the fortune. " '*True happiness is found in satisfying work.*' Fffft!"

"No, that's right!" Ron sat up and slapped my palm. "It's in the stars, in the cards, in the cookies—building the park is our work!"

It was late when I got home. Muttsy greeted me, for a change, without barking. The house was dark, except for a wedge of light under my parents' bedroom door. I could hear them talking as Muttsy and I went upstairs. Just then the telephone rang. "I'll get it!" I yelled.

My mom came into the hall. "You're home—good. Who could be calling at this hour?"

I picked up. "Hello?"

"Bronti?"

"Yeah?" I signaled my mom to go back to bed. "Who is this, *Thompson?* It's *late.*"

"I been thinking," Thompson said.

"How about thinking in the daytime? Seriously, man—"

His voice was low and breathy. "I been thinking about what's fair. I asked Freddy for a ticket that day first."

"So?"

"So you horned in and got *yours* first—the ticket that should have been mine."

"The order has nothing to do with it! I won because of the numbers I picked!"

"No, no, the winner was fated to buy a ticket exactly *at that moment.*"

"That's ridiculous. And so what? Even if it were true— *so what?*"

"You got my money."

"You're crazy. What do you expect me to do, hand it over to you?"

"Half," Thompson said quickly. "I'll settle for half."

"They warned me about nuisance phone calls," I sputtered, "but this is too much, man. See you around, unless I can avoid it. So long!" I hung up.

My mom popped out again. "Who was that?"

"Some guy," I said.

"Is something wrong?"

"No, I got rid of him." And just to make sure, after she closed her door, I took the receiver off the hook.

10

I got a lot of Z's that night, thanks to leaving the phone off the hook, and when I woke up and thought of Lennie Thompson, I laughed my head off. Give my money away? Sure, I was planning to give away some of it, but *half* to one nut because he thought he was *fated* to win my money? I got dressed and stashed my wallet and checkbook in my pocket. I was actually looking forward to going to school.

"Hi, how did you make out at the bank?" my mom asked as I came down to the kitchen. "Did you deposit it?"

"Yup," I said.

"So, back to the routine today. Is your homework done? Here, want some orange juice?"

Just then my dad squeezed by me in the doorway and took the glass from my mom. "Morning, Mike. I have to leave." He drank the juice. "How did it go at the bank yesterday?"

"Fine." I patted the pocket where my checkbook was. "Want to see what I got?"

"Later. I've got to go. Bud's waiting for me outside. If I

74

were you," he said to me, "I wouldn't carry evidence of your wealth around."

"Good luck today, Louis," my mom said. "He's got a tough week ahead," she explained to me. "The Americus Plaza deal is finally getting close to being wrapped up."

"Yeah? Good luck!" I repeated. "We've got it to burn around here."

"So *you* say." My dad reknotted his tie in front of the hall mirror. "Don't get tempted to dip into that account until we've seen Mercer. Okay, here goes everything, I hope. See you tonight."

My mom pushed down the toast in the toaster. "Dinner at six sharp tonight, Mike."

"Okay, but forget toast for me, I've got to be going."

"Without breakfast? Where are your books?"

"At school!"

"Who's walking Muttsy?"

"Could you?" I asked. "I want to get to school early." I knew she wouldn't argue with that.

I jogged the whole way to GHS, otherwise known as The Fortress, because the school looks like a castle and our teams are called the Green Knights. I felt like the Greenest Knight of all, carrying that wallet full of green stuff and hearing comments along the way from everybody who'd heard.

Inside the school, once I got there, there was even more attention. Kids who had been at my party pointed me out to everyone else. Someone yelled at me in the hall, "How about lending me five G's?" "Sure, call me," I said, and gave him the number of Glenfield State Bank.

When I got to my locker about eight, Sheila was already waiting for me. I didn't kiss her the way I usually do, because I felt funny with a crowd around. "Hi," I said, "see you later."

"When?" she asked. "At lunch? Can we sit together at lunch?"

"I told a *Glenhi Herald* reporter I'd give her an interview at lunch today. Hey, come on, Sheila, don't be sad—we're going to have *more* time together now."

The rest of the morning was one big production called "Everybody Wants to Be Buddies with Bronti." First a bunch of girls wanted to kiss me for luck—SMACK, SMACK! Then a guy—PSST, PSST—tried to sell me a gym bag full of pot, but I told him I was high enough without it. Meanwhile, all this time, pink-haired Mandy Calise was following me around through the halls—SIGH, SIGH—staring at me as if I were a rock star. Finally I was called into the office—HARRUMPH, HARRUMPH—by the principal, Lehman, who wanted to congratulate me and suggest that maybe now I could pay my class dues.

Right after that I saw Ron trying to get my attention in the corridor. He was waving another sketch of Brontisaurus Park. I yelled that I'd see him later, but he looked at me kind of disgusted. What did he think, that the park was the only thing I had on my mind?

It may sound as if I spent my whole day cruising, but I actually did go to classes. Most of my teachers knew about my win and wanted to hear the details. In English class Ryan had written on the board a quote from Robert Louis Stevenson: "The price we have to pay for money is paid in liberty."

"That's off the wall, Mr. Ryan," I said. "The main thing about money is, it *gives* you liberty."

Mr. Ryan's a good teacher, an ex-priest—bald, with a

fringe of red hair—that's why Ronnie and I always call him the Monk. The Monk loves to read aloud, so he gave himself an excuse, saying that because of my win, he wanted us to hear this Russian story about two guys in the last century who end up making a bet. The one, a rich old banker, says he'll give the poorer, younger guy two million rubles if the younger one stays as a voluntary prisoner in the banker's house for fifteen years.

"How much money was that?" everybody wanted to know.

"The value of the ruble would be different now," the Monk said. "Let's just say the younger man was convinced it would be worth it to become rich by giving up his freedom for fifteen years."

So—what does the prisoner *do* while he's in there? Does he last, does he end up getting the money? Read "The Bet" by Anton Chekhov if you want to find out. The ending is surprising and kind of strange, but I enjoyed hearing the Monk read it. Afterward we talked about money and freedom, and Ryan kept wanting to hear what I thought.

Would I make a bet like that? (A few kids in the class said sure, they'd do anything for two million.) I personally wouldn't give up my freedom for even one year. On the other hand, if money just *comes*, like mine did, without my having to give up anything, then how can it be bad? One kid said it was too early to tell what my money would do to me. I said why should it do anything? I'm still the same guy. A few kids laughed when I said that, because I'm known for being sort of a spendthrift. I pulled out my wallet and threw a couple of dollar bills in the air, which caused a big stir.

The Monk got us back on the track, though, discussing

whether money's the root of all evil. And then somebody asked if I thought my win meant that God was rewarding me. "I believe in God," I said, "but that's got nothing to do with lotteries. I figure God's got much more important stuff to do than decide who wins the weekly Pick-Six."

After English, on my way to math class, I suddenly felt something—a hairy arm around my neck, yanking my head back. "Ouch!"

Lingo chuckled and let go. "You'd be so easy to get. You need a bodyguard, Bronti, I'm not kidding. I'll be it!" he said. "Not for pay, just for the fun of it. All right?"

I rubbed my neck. Ouch. "Thanks for the offer, but it isn't necessary, man." We fell into step. "Who would bother a nice guy like me?" As we walked along—I had been thinking about this since lunchtime—I said to Lingo, "Feel like cutting out right now? Doing some shopping?"

His face lit up. "Sure, Mike."

That's the good thing about Lingo, no hemming and hawing. Just "Sure, Mike," like a kid. Sometimes it's nice to have an uncomplicated friend.

We had a ball on Main Street, Glenfield. I know there are better and bigger stores in the malls around here, but Main Street was the closest and I'd known these stores since I was a kid. I wasn't looking for anything in particular, I just felt like getting some small presents—cassette tapes for Lingo, an old *Star Trek* poster for Ronnie, flowers, which I had sent to my grandma and mom. I paid cash for most of the things, until I got to Medoff's Jewelers, where I bought Sheila a real pearl on a chain that I paid for by check.

All that walking made us hungry, so we stopped in at

Gucci's Pizza. In the past I'd always ordered it plain because it was cheap. Now I *knew* money made you free, as I ordered two Guccis with the works—one and a half for Lingo and the other half for me.

Coming out of Gucci's, I suddenly felt the urge to buy something major. Up until now I'd been kind of playing, ten bucks here, fifteen bucks there. "Where're we going next?" Lingo asked me, and I steered him two doors down. "You're kidding!" he exploded. "No, you're *serious*! Stenton Motors!"

Picture this: Frame one, a car salesman sees these two goofy teenagers. MUTTER, MUTTER you hear him grumbling as he starts to show them a beat-up heap. Frame two, Mike waves his lottery letter and his checkbook, and the salesman's expression changes. Frame three, Mike and his friend drive away, SNICKER, SNICKER, in a brand-new Rolls-Royce.

Okay, so I didn't buy a Rolls, but other than that, the picture's accurate. The salesman showed us Corvettes and Camaros and customized vans. I bopped around as if I knew cars, which I don't, examining everything on wheels and test-driving the ones that were in my top five. It wasn't easy, making a decision. Lingo loved all the sports cars. I had more or less promised Ronnie I was getting a van. I could have waited to decide, of course, but why wait when I had the money? Then I remembered Sheila saying "something sporty but comfortable." Hey, it was essential that Sheila be comfortable—I hoped we'd be spending prime time in my car. "I'll take the red Camaro," I decided, and wrote out a check for just under fifteen thousand dollars.

"Man, you did it!" Lingo pounded me while the salesman prepared the papers. "Yeah"—I beamed—"I only wish I could drive it away now." I couldn't pick it up until Saturday, a ridiculous test of my patience. "Don't tell anybody"—I made Lingo swear. "I want to surprise everyone."

When it was time to leave Stenton's, I got a great idea. Why walk? Call a cab! We dropped off Lingo, and then the rest of the way home I enjoyed fantasies of what it would be like to have my own car: PURR, PURR, VROOM, VROOM, WHOOOSH! ZOOOOOOM. SCREECH.

When I got home, I walked in bursting but determined to keep my secret. My parents were almost finished eating. "Hey, sorry, am I that late?"

"I told you six sharp," my mom murmured. "It's after seven. What *happened*?"

"Sorry. I got involved. I was doing some—business."

"Monkey business, I bet," my dad said.

I glanced at the table and saw that my mom had made one of my favorite meals—shell steaks, which by now looked like moccasins from L. L. Bean. "I had a great day—" I began, and then I remembered. "How about you, Dad? Did everything go all right?"

"It's still going on." He sawed his steak. "Damn, these things are ruined."

"I misjudged," my mom apologized. "I broiled them too long."

"How about giving them to Muttsy and going out to eat?" I suggested. Uh-oh, wrong thing to say. My mom can't stand wasting food.

My dad kept chewing determinedly. "You'd better save your money for postage, if you're intending to answer all that mail out there."

"What mail?"

"Out on the porch," my mom said. "By the way, the flowers you sent are in the living room. They're beautiful, Mike, thanks—"

"You're welcome." I went out on the porch. ZING! On the table was a carton loaded with mail. "This all came today?"

"Yes!"

"You're going to have to get your own phone," my dad called. "I put in a request to change our number to an unlisted one, but until it goes through, answer the phone!"

It began ringing that second, while I was thumbing through the envelopes: To Mike Bronti, The Bronti Fund, Mr. Mike Millionaire. "I'll get it!" I shouted, running back into the kitchen. "Hello, yes, this is Mike. No, I can't do that. I can't put up money to get a complete stranger out of jail. . . ." I had no sooner hung up than the doorbell rang and Muttsy started barking.

"This is driving me nuts." My dad got up. "Aren't we ever going to have any peace again around here?"

I opened the front door, and Muttsy growled at the sight of a deliveryman.

"United Parcel. Delivery for Mike Bronti. Eighteen packages for you. Sign here, sir. Is the dog dangerous?"

"No, she's a wimp."

My mom and dad came to the door. "What's this?"

"Must be my eighteen free gifts from the bank."

"What *are* they?" My mom and dad stared as the deliveryman staggered in with a huge pile of boxes.

Meanwhile the phone rang again, and at the same moment, old Muttsy struck. Either she thought the deliveryman was going to dognap her, or else she was offended that I'd called her a wimp. Anyway, she went after his ankles and then leaped and attacked the stack of cartons, so that they came crashing to the floor.

"I'd gladly give two million for some peace and privacy!" my dad howled above the noise.

11

Saturday morning, after almost a week of being a millionaire ... Had my money turned me evil yet? MIKE METAMORPHOSES INTO MISERLY MONSTER. BRONTI BECOMES BORING BRAGGART, BOASTING OF BUCKS. Nah, I was still the same lovable guy, a little busier than before—marking time in my room while I waited for my car to be ready at Stenton's.

By then my parents' number had been changed, and I had an answering machine hooked up to my very own phone so that the zillions of calls I'd been getting weren't driving my parents crazy. I pushed Rewind and then Play:

"THIS IS I. RONALD J. SCHWARTZ'S MACHINE SPEAKING TO MICHAEL T. BRONTI'S MACHINE. HOW ABOUT US TWO GETTING TOGETHER? WHO NEEDS HUMANS, ANYWAY? CALL ME, MIKE. IT'S IMPORTANT. IT HAS TO DO WITH NEXT YEAR."

After the beep I heard another voice.

"BRONTI? THIS IS LENNIE THOMPSON. PART OF THAT MONEY BELONGS TO ME!"

Thompson again. He'd been bugging me constantly. I pressed Fast Forward to get past him and tuned in the next message:

"THIS IS DONALD KALMAN FROM THE LOCAL OFFICE OF THE INTERNAL REVENUE SERVICE. I HAVE SOME INFORMATION REGARDING THE TAX SITUATION OF LOTTERY WINNERS. PLEASE CALL THE FOLLOWING NUMBER BETWEEN THE HOURS OF—"

I pushed Stop. Ignoring the other messages, I moved on to my mail.

Two full cartons had accumulated in less than a week. I tried to read some every day, but a lot of it was boring— from insurance companies, and stockbrokers, and burglar alarm salesmen, and banks. The letters to the fund were much more interesting. I got a kick out of reading them, actually. That's what I had sorted out now from the rest of the pile.

I opened one and looked at the swirly feminine handwriting: *Dear Mike, I saw you on TV and thought you looked adorable. I'm a freshman at Glenfield Community, and all my friends are going to Fort Lauderdale this year over spring break. I want to go, but I can't afford it. Then I got this idea. Maybe we could meet, and if we like each other we could go to Florida together? Enclosed is my picture. What do you think? Waiting to hear from you, Sally Dupre.* Sally Dupre . . . she looked amazingly like Sheila, I thought as I tucked the photograph in my desk drawer. Man, the possibilities were endless when you won the lottery.

I opened another envelope and read the letter. *Dear Mr. Bronti, I had a son who would be just your age now if he'd lived. He died a year ago, the victim of a driver who was drunk. I read somewhere that you're thinking of going to art school. My son, Peter, was also an aspiring artist. I wonder if you'd be interested in contributing to an art school scholarship in my son's name?*

I let it fall without reading the name and quickly opened another: *Dear Michele, you Granma and I was nabors yrs ago. You ask her about Mrs. Golpe, she tell you who I am. Now my husband lose a leg because his dibetic and we have only a little soc. security. I hate to ask, but we arnt eating so good and I hear about you have a fund* . . .

I put that one down, too, and stared at the pile. I hadn't realized there'd be so *many* and especially ones like those. I needed help, that was for sure, help making decisions and answering letters. I tried calling Lynne right then and there, but unfortunately she wasn't home.

I fell back on my pillow, paralyzed suddenly. Even if I gave away *all* my money, how many people could I help? Maybe my dad was right. The fund was impractical. No! I heard Amy protesting—that's a pitiful excuse! Amy. Oh, shoot, I had told Amy I'd come down to see her. I *would*, after I picked up my car.

Amy wouldn't approve of my car, I thought as I got ready to leave for Stenton's. *Fifteen thousand*, I could hear her saying, *just for a status symbol!* It would be more than that, I told myself. I could do good with it—drive my friends around, transport my grandma, and besides, with over two million dollars, wasn't it possible to help other people and have fun myself too? I went downstairs.

"Going out?" my mom asked me.

"Yeah, on an errand." I still figured it would be a blast to surprise them with the car. "Where's Dad?"

"Working. He's so exhausted, but he thinks the end is in sight for the Americus deal. I thought you were going down to Murray?"

"I'm going down there later. See you, good-bye!"

Walking over to Stenton Motors, I kept thinking about some of the fund letters. Amy had the right idea . . . So many people were hurting . . . Then I reached the lot and saw my Camaro—blazing red with black vinyl interior— and I decided fifteen thousand out of two million was a drop in the bucket. Man, it was something. I'd forgotten since I'd picked it out. How could anything that beautiful be anything but good? When I got behind the wheel and inhaled that new-car smell, I felt like I'd died and gone to heaven. I couldn't wait to show it off—who should I show it to first?

Sheila. No, my parents. No, *Ronnie*. No, Barry! I got the papers from the salesman who had registered the car for me and wrote him a final check. Also, my grandma would love to see what I'd bought. And Lynne would be interested. Or maybe Lingo should have the first look at it . . . I felt as if I was being pulled in at least eight directions as I VROOM-VROOMED out of the Stenton lot.

There was something about the Camaro—let's face it, it was sexy—something that made me forget everybody else and head straight for Sheila's house. I mean, my parents might not even like it. Ron might be mad that I hadn't bought a van. Barry might be jealous. But I was sure Sheila would love it. Maybe I could convince her to go away with me for a weekend now that I had a car. All the way over there my fantasies revolved around Sheila and me alone in it. If you're thinking my attraction was basically physical, there was some truth to that.

I tooled across town in the Camaro with the volume up on the stereo. Woooooweeee! Watch it, though—LUCKY LOTTERY LAD LOSES LICENSE. Wouldn't want that to happen. This was freedom. Having your own wheels, going to show 'em to your woman. "You're my woman," I sang under my breath as I pulled up in front of Sheila's. I parked and went to the door, where I impatiently rang the bell.

Within seconds Sheila opened up. "Mike! Oh, wow, Mike, what a surprise! How did you get here? Did you walk?"

"No, I drove." Grinning, I entered her house.

"Is that *Mike?*"

"Our big winner!"

Suddenly Sheila's parents were there in the hall, her dad shaking my hand, her mom kissing me. It was the first time they'd ever greeted me in any way like that. Pretty nice, being a celebrity.

Her dad led me into the family room. "What does it feel like, being a millionaire?"

"Now, Sam, he's still Sheila's Mike," her mom clucked. "Don't embarrass the poor boy."

"Poor! How do you like that—poor! Come on, Mike, sit here—make yourself at home."

Sheila looked great. Her hair was clean and smelled lemony. She was wearing a scoop-neck lavender sweater and a string of fake pearls that I'd bought her at K Mart when I was a nobody—a poor boy. No question about it, I was thinking as her dad made jokes and her mom got me a soda, you got treated better when you were rich. I just hoped they'd eventually leave the two of us alone.

"So is this win going to change your plans?" Mrs. Cooke asked as I was sipping my soda. "Sheila said you were thinking of going to California."

"I can't permit that," Mr. Cooke kidded me. "That money should be spent here."

"Dad belongs to the Glenfield Chamber of Commerce," Sheila said to me. "Their slogan is 'Spend in Glenfield.' "

"Well, you should be happy," I told her dad. "I spent a big chunk of it here today. I've got something outside to show."

"What?" Sheila jumped up, like a kid who's been waiting all year for Santa Claus.

"Come on." I got up and headed for the door again, and all three of them followed me outside.

"Yours? Mike! I love it!" Sheila scrambled into the front seat of the Camaro.

"Handsome car." Mr. Cooke looked at the license plate. "Bought here at Stenton's? Can't do better than that."

"It's gorgeous," Mrs. Cooke said. "Almost as gorgeous as the two of you in it."

By then I had gone around and gotten in behind the wheel. "I'm going to show Sheila how it rides," I said, waving to her parents. It was nice being their hero, but I wanted some time with Sheila alone. They looked a little bit surprised as we pulled away and waved again, but they were smiling, and why not? Their daughter had hooked up with a lucky guy. "Where shall we go?" I asked Sheila.

"Let's show the car to Sunny and Billy. They've been dying to meet you."

More relatives. "Not today," I said. "Let's do that another time. Let's drive out in the country, just the two of us—we've never had the chance before." All my old fantasies came rushing back. This was going to be a great day.

And it was, let me tell you. We stopped at my house to show my parents the Camaro, but neither of them was home, so I just pocketed the real pearl I had bought as a surprise for Sheila, and then we went on. The weather was good, the Camaro was comfortable. "This is exactly the car I hoped you'd get," Sheila said. We drove out beyond

Glenfield, where there's some nice scenery, and we parked for a long while. Sheila's hair brushed my cheek, her cologne filled my nostrils, her lips met mine and stayed there. Maybe, with more time and luck, I could get her to be a less old-fashioned girl.

When the sun began to go down, I got an idea. "Let's end this day right by having dinner at the Top o' the Port."

"Are you serious?"

"Would I kid you?" I said, kissing her on the ear. The Top o' the Port is Glenfield's best restaurant, much too expensive for my parents. Barry would flip when I told him later I'd been to the Top o' the Port.

"Are we dressed right?" Sheila looked down at her skirt and my sweater and corduroys.

Sheila always worries about stuff like that. "What do you think," I moaned, "they're going to toss out a millionaire? If we've got the money, they have to let us in. It's a free country, right?"

When we got to the restaurant, we left the car with one of those parking attendants.

"He's looking funny at us," Sheila said. "We should be wearing better clothes."

"Come on, relax!" I insisted. "As long as you have the bucks, they'll let you in this place nude!" We got into a glass elevator and rode all the way to the top.

The restaurant was really something, hot and cool at the same time. Cool, with its chrome and mirrors, but warm with gray carpeting that went across the floor and up the walls. It was very rich and quiet, with windows everywhere overlooking the airfield and lots of flashing lights outside on the runways and on the planes.

"Good evening, sir." A stiff-necked guy in a black tuxedo greeted us. He looked down his nose at me as if I *were* nude. "Your name, please? Do you have a reservation?"

Reservation? "Uh, we don't have one. I'm Mike Bronti."

He looked at me blankly. "We require reservations, Mr. Bratty, did you say?"

"Bronti," I said with emphasis. I guess my fame hadn't traveled as far as Top o' the Port. Remembering movies I'd seen, though, I took out my wallet and, flashing my bills, I coolly handed the guy a twenty-buck bribe.

He made it disappear into his pocket, like a magician. "You'll need *this,* sir," he said, "we require it." Then he held out a suit jacket for me to put on over my sweater, and he led us quickly by some other customers to an out-of-the-way table.

I stopped before we got there, though, at a better table and slipped him another ten without Sheila seeing me, so that when we were seated she smiled. "I'm so happy, Mike. This is perfect."

"It's so *rich,"* Sheila whispered after he'd left and the waiter had brought us our menus. "Look, there aren't any prices. How do we know what everything costs?"

"There're prices on mine." I pointed. "Order whatever you want. You're not supposed to worry about the cost." It was good I'd seen a lot of old movies, otherwise I wouldn't have known how to act in this place. Sheila ordered shrimp cocktail and filet mignon, but I decided on snails and frogs' legs. Hell, this was supposed to be one of the ad-ventures of our lives.

While we were waiting for the food, I filled her in on what had been happening. I told her about some of the people who'd been calling me and about getting all that mail. I made a point of not mentioning that Lynne had offered to help me with it. For some reason Sheila gets upset whenever she hears Lynne's name.

After a while the waiter came back and set our first courses in front of us. "Oooh!" Sheila said when she saw her giant shrimp. Then she looked at my snails. "Mike, come on, you aren't *eating* those!"

"Why not?"

She blinked. "How will you swallow them? They look like rocks!"

She thought I was intending to eat the shells, so I pretended I was. She stared at me wide-eyed, and then at the last minute I put the shell down and pulled out the edible part with my cocktail fork and held it up in the air.

"Gross!" Sheila winced. "It looks like a slug!"

It was good, even a slug would be, drowned in all that garlic and butter, but Sheila had a point. The things *did* look like slugs. Somewhere here there was a cartoon idea, I thought, but I was too busy eating to work it out.

"Filet mignon?" the waiter was saying. "And, sir, your frogs' legs are ready."

"How are they?" Sheila asked skeptically as I munched on a crispy leg.

"Delicious," I exaggerated. I was paying a lot and they ought to be good, but the truth was they tasted a lot like Beefarama chicken nuggets.

While we were finishing our main course, Sheila gradually got very quiet. Playing with her K Mart pearl necklace, she said, "You know, since this happened to you, a lot of girls are wishing they were me."

I smiled. "Yeah?"

But Sheila wasn't smiling. She looked as if I'd lost my last buck.

"Hey, come on, finish eating!" Then I noticed tears in her eyes. "What's wrong?"

"Mike"—her voice broke and she tugged at her pearls again—"how long—how long do you think this'll go on?"

"What?"

"All these *people* hanging around you!"

I swallowed my last bite. "What's wrong with that?"

"I'm happy about the money"—her bottom lip quivered—"but I'm afraid, Mike, I'm afraid!"

"Of *what?*"

She covered her face. "Of what's going to happen to *us*, now that every girl in Glenfield is after you!"

Was that true? "Nothing bad's going to happen." I cleared my throat. "We'll go places like this together more often, that's all. We'll go away for weekends . . ." I suggested cautiously, but Sheila didn't seem to hear.

"It's going to keep *on* like this, I know it," she continued, "with other girls wishing they were me, until one of them *is*! Mandy Calise told somebody she'd do *anything* for you!"

Anything? Hmmm. "Mandy Calise is a flake."

"Maybe *she* is," Sheila stammered, "but the money's going to bring you so many *temptations*. You're going to end up being busier than before, when you worked with that *Lynne*! We'll see each other less and less, I *know* it! You'll go to California—"

"But I'll come back!"

"You think you will, but you won't." Her tears spilled over then, and she turned her face away. Then she looked at me again. "I'm sorry, Mike. Don't be mad at me. It's just that I love you so much!"

"Me, too," I said, fumbling in my pocket for the pearl

from Medoff's Jewelers. It was just what was needed to make those tears disappear. I was about to pull it out and tell her that nothing would come between us when the waiter appeared and asked, "Coffee or dessert, sir?" So to get rid of him I ordered us coffee and two gooey parfaits.

As soon as he left I took out the box. "Sheila," I said, "here's a surprise for you."

Sheila sat up and blinked her tears back as the waiter served our parfaits. Over a mountain of whipped cream she gazed at me. "For me, Mike? What is it?"

"A present, to show you you've got nothing to worry about. To show you I'm thinking about you even when I'm not with you." I handed over the box.

She opened it. "Mike, a *real* pearl? Oh, it's so beautiful!"

"Not as beautiful as you are," I said. It was as if being rich had turned me into this suave romantic guy. I reached over, across both our desserts, to help her undo the cheap pearls she was wearing, and what happened from then on is kind of fuzzy in my mind.

Sheila, excited and nervous, was holding the real pearl in one hand, but she was also trying to help me take off the old necklace, and she pulled on it too hard. The next thing I knew, the K Mart necklace had broken, and little fake pearls were flying everywhere. "Oh, no!" Sheila wailed, jumping up out of her seat.

I dived and grabbed, first like an infielder after a couple of line drives. Then I went for the grounders. Little fake pearls were on the tablecloth, in the saucers, and on the carpet. The waiter and the guy in the tux came rushing to our sides. "May we be of some assistance?" both of them asked us at once.

"I'm so embarrassed!" Sheila moaned. Other customers

must have been turning around, because she kept saying over and over, "Mike, take me home!"

I couldn't see who was doing what at first. I was too busy fishing for fake pearls on the floor, where a lot of them had fallen and rolled pretty far. Then, under the table, I met the waiter. Eyeballing each other, we both held out our cupped hands. *I have more pearls than you have!* I felt like saying. *Ha, ha, ha, ha!* I was just beginning to see the incident for its humor and was about to get up and comfort Sheila when she let out a sound I have to describe as a shriek.

"Iiiiiieeee! Nooo!"

I leaped to her side, pretty certain an airplane had crash-landed. The ceiling was still there, though. "What's the matter?" I asked.

Sheila pointed to her dessert, where I could see a sinkhole in the whipped cream. In her excitement she had dropped the pearl from Medoff's deep into her parfait.

"Don't worry," I tried to calm her, "we'll get it, we'll get it." I gazed down into the tall glass, trying to see the end of the chain.

"Allow me, sir," the guy in the tux said, and with another magicianlike gesture he thrust three fingers into the whipped cream and came up with the pearl. With an absolutely straight face he dropped it into a napkin and said, "Would you care to sit down, sir and madam, while I take care of this and bring you your check?"

I would have been glad to, but Sheila couldn't. She was beet-red and sniffling, and I figured the best thing to do would be to take her to get her coat. The magician was incredibly fast, though. He was back in a flash with the real pearl, cleaned up, and he handed Sheila an envelope, into which the waiter and I dumped the fake pearls.

"Your check, sir," the magician said.

I examined it and took out my wallet. One hundred twenty bucks they wanted. I gave him two hundred. "Keep the change."

Both the waiter and the guy in the tux stared. "Thank you, sir. *Thank* you."

"Don't mention it," I replied. "I was a waiter once myself."

It took a while to calm Sheila down, even after we were back in the Camaro. "I was so clumsy! So embarrassed! You'll probably never want to take me out again!"

"Sure I will," I insisted. "It could have happened to anyone." I was back to thinking it was funny, but naturally I didn't say that. Instead I sighed. I'd been hoping for passion, at this point, at the end of the evening. I was thinking in terms of breaking in the Camaro, that is, making tonight—shall we say—OUR FIRST TIME. Now the mood was pretty well broken. Only an insensitive clod would have pushed it. So I drove Sheila home without stopping until we parked in front of her house.

Even then I could tell she was too upset to switch the mood to romance and passion, so I just patted her hand gently and kept saying everything was all right.

"You're just saying that."

"I mean it! What's the big deal? You got your good pearl back."

"I know. I love it, but whenever I wear it now, I'll think of—whipped cream!"

I put my arm around her. "So what?"

Suddenly she hugged me very tightly, so tightly that for a second I had hopes again. "I have to go in now," she said though. "Mike, will you promise—?"

"Promise what?"

She motioned for me to come around and open her door. "Promise you'll never leave me?" she whispered as we walked toward her house, hand-in-hand. "Promise you won't let the money pull us apart?"

"Why would it?"

"Just *promise.*"

"Yeah, sure—I promise."

She smiled and fell against me. "Good! Oh, Mike, I feel much better. I'd die if anything happened between us. I love you so much—good night!"

12

     After I left Sheila off and was driving home alone, I kept hearing her voice again: *I love you* . . . I loved her, too—the smell of her hair and the taste of her whipped-cream-flecked lips. Ridiculous of her to be worrying. Why would I leave her? I'd *take her with me* to California. Just thinking about it raised my temperature. Beads of sweat popped out on my forehead, the size of K Mart fake pearls.

Hey, whoop-de-doo! I remembered as I turned into Court Street. What a kick it was going to be to show my parents my car. If they were upstairs already, I'd drag them outside in their bathrobes. No need. The living room lights were on, which meant they still must be up. While I was parking at the curb, I noticed another car stopped ahead of me, with someone in the driver's seat. Suddenly it pulled away in a cloud of exhaust. Weird. I watched for a second and then went into my house, where Muttsy was waiting at the door. "Hi!" I called.

"Hi."

I went into the living room, where my parents were sitting stiffly at opposite ends of the sofa. "Was somebody here? Did somebody just leave?" I asked.

"No," my mom said. "Why?"

"This car just pulled away out there—" *Car*. I could hardly say the word without grinning.

"Where have you been?" my mom asked now.

"Out with Sheila. We ended up at the Top o' the Port." I was exploding with the news of the car, but something made me hold off.

"The Top o' the Port?" my mom repeated. "I thought you were going to visit Amy. She called—she spent her whole day waiting for you."

Damn. So *stu*pid! I had completely forgotten about Amy and going down to Murray State. "Oh, wow." I clicked my teeth. "I got tied up with Sheila, and I guess I—I forgot to call Ames."

"Tied up doing what?" My dad spoke for the first time now, his voice husky, as if he'd been sleeping.

Driving around, I was about to say, but I kept my mouth shut. Were they annoyed at me because of the Amy thing? Had they heard about my car from somebody else, so that they were hurt I hadn't told them first? My dad was staring strangely at a loose thread on the couch. "Is anything wrong?" I asked.

My mom glanced at my dad, as if giving him a chance to speak first, but when he didn't, she looked at me. "Dad's Americus Plaza deal fell through today."

"Fell through? How could that be? I thought it was all sewed up . . ."

"Just because *you're* having a run of luck," my dad said, "don't think everybody is. What happened today was crazy— Hell, what's the use of discussing it? The client completely changed his mind." My dad hugged his arms as if he were cold. "More than six months I put into this thing. It would have guaranteed my income for a year."

"Well, the money's no problem," I told him. "And you'll sell it eventually, right?"

"No, I won't." My dad shifted and sat up stiffly again. "Bud's given Americus to somebody else. I've been sent down to the minors, you could say—reassigned to a couple of white elephants that have been on the market since the year one."

"But with your twenty-three years of experience, Lou," my mom began, "you'll sell—"

"No, I won't!" he said impatiently. "Those years are the *problem*, not the solution. It's the young guys who're striking the deals. I've been in the business too long."

"So get out of it," I told him, finally taking off my jacket. "Money's no problem now. Quit and do something else."

My dad looked at me as if I was suggesting he jump off a bridge or something.

"It's worth thinking about, Lou," my mom said. "I've felt for the last couple of years that you'd be happier in a job with less pressure."

"What are you talking about?" my dad snapped. "I can take whatever pressure Bud decides to lay on! Let's get some sleep," he said suddenly. "Come on, let's go up."

"Right," my mom agreed. "Things'll probably look clearer in the morning. Mike, there's more mail for you." She and my dad got up creakily, as if they'd been sitting there for a long time. "Look in the hall, something came from Cummings Institute."

"Yeah?" I dove for the box in the hallway and found the Cummings letter. "It's fat!" I ripped it open. " 'We are pleased to inform you have been accepted' . . . All *right!*"

"Congratulations." My mom hugged me. "I'll read what it says in the morning. It's definite? You're accepted?"

I read the rest of the letter quickly. "Yeah. I have to send in a deposit within two weeks, to reserve my place. I wonder if Ron got in. He left me a message, but he didn't mention Cummings. I'll call him."

"Not tonight you won't," my dad said. "No more calls. It's too late. Congratulations." Then he patted my arm as he passed to head up the stairs. "Looks like you've got the world by the tail. Have you done anything about seeing Phil Mercer yet?"

"No, I will. I've been so swamped—"

"He doesn't even have time to see Amy!" my mom said, sounding annoyed as she followed my dad upstairs.

"I'll call her," I promised. "I'll see her next weekend."

My mom paused halfway up. "Grandma's been wanting to see you too. Maybe we can pick her up and go to church together tomorrow."

"Sure."

"Good night," my parents said in unison. "Lock the door," my mom added.

Hey wait! Don't go up yet! I felt like yelling. *I've got this fantastic car outside!*

"I'm really dragging," I heard my dad say to my mom.

It was obvious they both were wiped out. I'd wait and show my car in the morning, when they'd be much more ready to appreciate it. I'd drive to church. What a kick— driving people around in *my* car.

When Muttsy and I went up to my room, my parents were talking behind their closed door. I couldn't hear the exact words, but I could tell my mom was trying to cheer up my dad. He can be moody sometimes. It's hard to believe he's the son of my grandma. I must have inherited *her* personality. Okay, so he was disappointed about losing a deal, but why wouldn't he want to take a chance and start doing something else?

Tired as I was after a big day, I didn't feel ready for sleeping. I kept thinking of Sheila and wishing she were with me right then. I was still wound up over my car, too, and my acceptance from Cummings. I felt like calling a few people, but my parents might hear me, so I flopped down on my bed and listened to the day's messages on my machine.

"MIKE? I SHOULD HAVE KNOWN."

Amy's message was the first one.

"I GAVE UP A BIG MEETING THIS MORNING SO I'D BE HERE WHEN YOU CAME DOWN. A LOT OF PEOPLE WANT TO SEE YOU, THERE'RE IMPORTANT THINGS I HAVE TO TELL YOU. CALL ME AS SOON AS POSSIBLE, UNLESS YOU'VE ALREADY JOINED THE ENEMY—THE CALIFORNIA SUN-WORSHIPERS AND GOOF-OFFS."

I felt bad. I really did. Amy had a right to be mad at me. While I was listening to the next message, I wrote out a check to her group. A thousand dollars ought to help them. I'd give them more later on, after I went down there next weekend and met them in the flesh.

"BRONTI? HOW COME YOU DON'T ANSWER MY CALLS, MAN?"

I pressed Fast Forward. Lennie Thompson again. What a pain in the neck.

"MIKE THE MILLIONAIRE? YOUR HUMBLE SERVANT, SCHWARTZ, HERE—"

It was Ron, putting on a voice, like an oriental servant in an old movie.

"DO MY EYES DECEIVE ME? TODAY I AM WALKING ON MAIN

STREET AND I SEE HIS ROYAL RICHNESS DRIVING WHEELS. THEY'RE *YOURS*? WHY DIDN'T YOU TELL YOUR HUMBLE SERVANT? WHAT HAPPENED TO THE VAN PLAN? MY DRAWINGS FOR BRONTI-SAURUS PARK BECOME MORE INSPIRED BY THE MINUTE, BUT—BRONTI, YOU BASTARD, CALL ME! DID YOU GET INTO CUMMINGS? *I* DID."

Great. I knew he would if I had, but it was nice all the same. I got undressed and ready for bed, still listening to my messages. There were a couple from salesmen, including Barry, who was still on his townhouse kick. A few calls were from strangers, even though I had publicized that people should *write* to the fund. The last one was the best:

"MIKE BRONTI? YOU DON'T KNOW ME YET, BUT WE GOT SOMETHING MAJOR IN COMMON. WHEN I SAW YOU ON TV FOR WINNING THE LOTTERY, I SAID, 'HEY, THAT'S *ME*!' AND THE TRUTH FINALLY CAME OUT. I'M YOUR TWIN BROTHER, SEPARATED AT BIRTH. IF YOUR (OUR!) PARENTS DENY THIS, THEY'RE LYING. I'M SURE YOU'LL BE WANTING TO SHARE WHAT YOU WON WITH YOUR OWN FLESH AND BLOOD. MY NAME IS TONY SOLO (REALLY BRONTI). I'LL BE TRYING TO CALL YOU AGAIN REAL SOON. WHAT LUCK THAT I FOUND YOU. TAKE IT EASY, BRO!"

I fell asleep laughing.

"*Mike*, it's almost time to leave for church," my mom shouted upstairs in the morning. "Have you spoken to Amy?"

"I will now." I tried calling her, but she wasn't in her room. The car. Show my parents the *car*, I thought as I got up and put my clothes on. I'd give my dad a whirl around the block and take my grandma and mom to church.

"I've got something to show you," I said right away, as soon as I went downstairs. My dad looked up from the

Sunday paper. My mom put down her cup. "I was dying to show you last night, but I figured this morning you could see better. Come on outside." My dad seemed reluctant, but my mom was curious. I opened the front door. "Tada!" I announced. "The Camaro—it's mine!"

"Yours? It's gorgeous, Mike, but when?" My mom grinned as we walked toward it. "How did you buy it so quickly? It's always taken Dad and me six months to make up our minds about a car."

"We had no choice," my dad said as we passed his five-year-old station wagon. "We always had plenty of time to decide while we saved up the money."

Both of them climbed into the Camaro and asked a bunch of questions. My mom liked it. My dad did too, I suppose, but his mind seemed to be on other things. "How about going for a ride in it this afternoon?" I suggested.

"Sure, fine," he said.

Then my mom and I picked up my grandma, who went crazy over the Camaro. "Beeootiful!" she kept saying. "I like the red. I'm glad you got red. It rides *nice*. Your daddy likes it? You should lend him, when he has customers."

"I will," I said as we went into church.

I was glad for a short timeout at St. Joseph's, where I'd gone since I was a kid. The atmosphere was just what I needed after a hectic week of being a millionaire. The sun was shining through the stained glass, lighting up certain pieces like jewels. Some of my best artwork ever, I'd drawn right here, copying the figures on the windows. On this day the priest—did he know about my win?—spoke about not letting yourself become too materialistic, too attached to things of this world. Not that I felt guilty or anything, but when they took up the collection, I hurriedly made out my second check of the day for one thousand bucks, to St. Joseph's Church.

After mass, my mom and I drove my grandma and a couple of her friends home. "Oooooo!" they all giggled. "Such a nice car!" "And a nice *kid*, too," my grandma informed them. "He's not one of those who only thinks about—*materials*. Generous? You shoulda seen the flowers he sent me the other day! Tell 'em, Mike, how good you are."

I didn't say a word. Funny, I loved to impress Barry, and the guys at Freddy's, and snobby waiters, but in front of certain other people it seemed tacky to show off.

When my mom and I got home, my dad was reading the paper. Or rather, he was sitting in a chair with the real estate section in his lap.

"Lunch'll be ready in a minute," my mom said.

"Want to take a spin around the block meanwhile?" I asked my dad.

"Okay." He hoisted himself out of his chair. "Okay, may as well."

Suddenly I felt bad for my dad. He was coming with me now mainly to be nice to me—to show me he liked my new car even though his wasn't as nice. Must be tough, losing a deal when you were used to being the top guy. I knew how it felt—I'd lost out myself on a couple of things, like drawing competitions that Ronnie had won. "Want to drive it?" I asked, after I'd opened the doors on both sides.

"No, thanks," he said. "It's yours. Give me a quick tour."

We had a good ride around Glenfield, and my dad seemed to relax a little, enough so that I risked bringing up the subject again. "Don't worry about the Americus thing," I told him. "Now that I won, we have plenty of money."

"It's *your* money, Mike."

"It's *ours!* The family's! We could start a business to-gether."

"What kind of business"—he half smiled—"selling comic books? Look, I don't want to be a kill-joy. I'm trying hard not to be, but—your luck and your money are yours and my problems are mine."

"I thought we were a family! You're always saying that!"

"We are. Listen, if I was sick or something, it'd be different. As it is, I'm still kicking, so you don't have to rush to the rescue yet. Do yourself a favor, though. Don't put off seeing Mercer and our lawyer, Tom DeAngelo. You need some expert advice on how to invest, and I trust both of them. Let me make you an appointment, okay?"

"Don't worry," I told him. "I'll do it myself."

Later on that day I asked my mom, "Why won't Dad let me set him up in a business?"

"It's a matter of pride right now," she said. "He wants to try to solve his own problems, I guess. Let's try to be patient."

I was patient, I *was*—that day and the days that followed. If he was moody, I told myself it was because of his bad break. I didn't expect him to be as excited about my car and about Cummings as I was, but he could have at least been as patient with me as I was being with him!

Patient in the matter of *math,* is what I'm talking about. The next day, unfortunately, a progress report arrived from my math teacher, Mr. Chu. Math has always been my worst subject, plus, since the lottery win, I had cut class a few times. I was in danger of failing, the progress report said.

In *danger,* that's all it said, but my dad blew it up out of proportion. "No more cutting!" he ordered. "And I want that homework done!"

"*Okay,*" I agreed. "I don't see why it's such a big deal, though, especially now that I've been accepted—"

"Accepted! You think an acceptance means you don't have to bother doing any more work? Your acceptance is contingent on graduating. It says that right in the letter."

"I *know,*" I insisted. "Don't worry, I won't flunk anything. Give me a break, can't you? It's not every day a guy wins over two million bucks!"

That night I went up to my room and filled out my acceptance card to Cummings. It had to be returned, along with a deposit, otherwise they'd give somebody else my place. I wrote the check and put the envelope on my desk, along with some fund letters that had just come in. *Dear Mike, I heard about you and hope you can help me. All my friends have more money than I have, and they buy these expensive designer clothes. All I'm asking for is one outfit (any designer) and one Gucci bag—*

Ugh. I went on to the next one. *Dear Mr. Bronti, Goodheart is an organization that grants last wishes to terminally ill children . . .* From the most ridiculous requests to the most pitiful—they were still coming in. I called Lynne and read her a few, which took up a good part of the evening. Then I phoned Sheila and told her how much I'd missed her all day. I meant to do my math and some drawing and call Ron and Amy, but there wasn't enough time. When I let Muttsy out, I noticed a car cruising by my house again. Don't be paranoid, I told myself, and I went up to bed.

That night I had a dream that my dad was in a prison or someplace, and it was essential that I get there if his life was going to be saved. I guess the dream made a big impact, because I kept thinking about it the next day in school and feeling that in real life I'd like to do something nice for my dad.

His birthday was coming, I realized while I was doodling in history class. Thursday. Suddenly I got a brainstorm about how I could make it a day he'd never forget. From then on I couldn't concentrate, so I figured, what was the use of sitting in school? My dad didn't want me to cut, but what I was about to do I was doing for *him.* So after history I took off. Ron saw me as I was sneaking out.

"Holy hell, man, where have you been?" He came after me. "Where're you hanging out these days, at Rich Guys Anonymous?"

"No! Hey, I got accepted!" I pounded him on the back. "Congratulations! I've been meaning to return your messages, but I've been so damned busy. California, here we come!"

"What about that car I saw? It's yours?"

"Yeah. Look, it'll be fine for—"

"You said a *van,* man . . ."

"The Camaro's beautiful!"

Ron looked hurt. "Yeah, but we could've transported stuff in it, slept in it. . . . When can we get together? I've got maps to show you. How about after school today?"

"No, sorry, I'm going to be busy. I'm doing this thing for my dad."

He tweaked his mustache and looked at me worriedly, like a Muttsy, afraid of being abandoned. "You're not changing your mind, are you?"

"About the park? No, definitely not. . . ." I still *was* interested, very. But even if I hadn't been, I wouldn't have admitted it. He was counting on this thing. We had planned a park for years. I couldn't let him down.

So I left school and made my rounds, setting up my dad's birthday surprise. It took a long time, because I wanted to plan the whole thing just right. First I had to keep in mind what he would like—my dad wasn't into showing off. And then for *me* it was important that the presentation be perfect. I did it, all in that one day. Everything was set up. Whooooee! It cost me a bundle. But it would certainly be worth it to cheer my dad up.

He needed it. He really did. My mom admitted to me she was worried. Dad had made an appointment to show his white elephant and the client never came. He was trying to keep up a good front at home, but the call from school didn't help matters. Mr. Chu contacted my dad to tell him I'd cut again.

"I can't believe it!" my dad bellowed. "Is this what the money's doing to you? Is this how you respect your parents?"

I took it bravely, like Muttsy, with my tail between my legs. I couldn't tell him yet that I had cut in order to do something for *him*.

Thursday night came. I had told my mom in advance that I had arranged a surprise for after dinner. We had talked about taking Dad out, but I decided the presentation would be better at home. Mom made dinner and a cake. Dad cracked jokes, trying to be upbeat, but unfortunately they weren't that funny. It was obvious he was just putting up a cheerful front. I had a hard time keeping cool while we ate. This certain person was coming at seven, and I kept glancing at my watch. Finally, looking out the window, I saw headlights and I jumped up from the table.

The bell rang. "I'll get it." I opened the door. "Hi. Dad, can you come here a minute? There's something for you out here."

"Out where?"

"Here!" By now I was ready to have a heart attack. I handed my mom her coat and pulled my dad by the elbow.

"Come on, Lou," my mom urged him.

I led them down the steps, with Muttsy behind us—down the path to the curb. "Happy birthday!"

"What's this?" my dad asked.

"A Cutlass station wagon." I grinned. "It's all yours. Do you like it?"

My parents looked at each other and then at the driver who had delivered it.

"Some surprise, huh?" he said.

We were all watching my father.

"Like it?" I asked him again.

His mouth twitched. "Mike, I can't let you do this. You can take it back, can't you?" He looked desperately at the driver.

"Why?" I asked. "If you don't like the color or something, I arranged it so you can switch."

"We can even change models," the driver said.

"No, it's not that," my dad said huskily. "I'm sorry, but I *can't*." He looked at me in the dim light. "Mike, I understand what you were trying to do, but I already *have* a car."

"It's five years old!" I argued. "It'll help, maybe with your clients. It'll be fun! It's nice, isn't it? Isn't it a great station wagon?"

"You didn't pay for it yet, did you?" he asked, ignoring me.

"Yes, I paid for it! Another color, then, another model—a sedan or a hatchback . . ."

Shaking his head, he looked at the driver. "My son can get his money back?"

The driver shrugged. "You haven't taken title yet. I'll have to ask my boss."

"I'm sure he will, under the circumstances. I'd appreciate it . . ."

"Dad, it's your birthday present!" My eyes stung. I felt like I couldn't breathe. "Why not *enjoy* it?" I asked him. "You're making a dumb mistake!"

"It wouldn't be the first one."

"I don't get it, Dad." I bit my cheeks.

He reached out and grabbed my hand, but I pulled it away from him. "Let me try to explain—" he began.

But I didn't want to hear his explanation. "Forget it!" I said angrily, and hurried into the house.

13

Picture a guy, really proud, picking out a mind-blowing present for his father, and then when he gives it, the father acts as if the guy has goofed in some way. Not so funny, huh? Not quite right as comic-strip material. . . . What was *wrong* with giving him a new station wagon? I listened impatiently to his reasons when he came back into the house.

Too much money to spend on a present, he told me. And it would be obvious to people at work that I'd paid for it.

"So what?"

He appreciated my generosity, he said, but he preferred to keep a low profile just now. I'd spent enough on my own car, he went on. How much had I spent by this time, anyway? And didn't I realize that I would have to pay more taxes and that I needed to make investments? After twenty years my lottery money would stop. And on top of that—where *was* my money? In a *checking* account? He'd told me to put it in high-interest *savings*. I should see Mercer immediately and switch to a money market fund, he said.

I was too upset even to argue with him. It was as if he

111

was *going out of his way* to be miserable. A new car might have made him more successful, or at least made him feel good. He could have sold the old one and used the money. Instead of enjoying my luck, he was acting like it was a punishment, and he wasn't only hurting himself, he was taking the fun away for the rest of us!

As usual, my mom tried to smooth things over. She said I shouldn't take the rejection *personally*. How else could I take it? I'd been so happy, being able to afford to buy him a car. My dad apologized for hurting my feelings, but I still felt really rotten. Finally, though, we agreed to try to respect each other's point of view.

On his side, that supposedly meant he would treat me less like an irresponsible kid. On my side, it meant accepting that he didn't want expensive presents or money from me. What they expected, my parents said, was for me to quit celebrating and get back to normal. The trouble was, trying to enjoy life to the fullest *was* normal for me.

I compromised, I guess you'd say. I kept going out, now that I could afford it—mostly with Sheila, but also with the guys, and some friends of Barry. I usually paid. What's money for? If *they* got lucky and I was broke, they'd pay for *me*. At the same time, though, I did some math so I wouldn't flunk. I hired a cleaning service for my parents, so they'd stop bugging me about my room. And I went to Phil Mercer for financial advice.

"I spoke to your dad and he agrees," Mercer said, loading me up with boring brochures. "We suggest going with tax-free bonds, or blue-chip stocks, or CDs."

ZZZZZZ, boring. I guess he thought I would decide right then how I was going to tie up my money, but when I told him I wasn't sure, he said, "Okay, take some more time.

Shift your money into a money market fund, meanwhile. Do yourself a favor."

"Okay," I agreed, just to keep him quiet. I liked having the money within reach, where I could get a few hundred dollars if I needed it. Once it was tied up in accounts with stupid initials, I might as well be my old poor self again.

So, with my money still in the checking account, I marked my one-month anniversary. One month of being New Jersey's youngest lottery millionaire! I was loving every minute of it, from seeing my face on a billboard ad to being gawked at by women at school, especially good old pink-haired Mandy Calise. Most of my teachers kidded around with me about my money and seemed to expect me to goof off a little. Five banks sent me credit cards without my even having to apply. Barry DeVane was starting to be impressed with me. Lingo by now had become my shadow. Only Ronnie . . . I don't know, Ronnie acted strange sometimes, as if he was hurt that I wasn't spending more time with him alone.

How could I, though, with all my other friends, and my mail and messages, and seeing Sheila? Things were going pretty well with Sheila and me. Just a matter of time now, I figured, until she'd agree to go away with me alone. I also mentioned about her coming to California with me, and she got really excited. "Sunny and Billy are thinking about going to California on their honeymoon!" she said. "Mike, you've got to meet them!" "Sure, anytime," I told her.

It was hard arranging these things, though. I'm embarrassed to admit that for four Saturdays I had put off going to see Amy at Murray State. Every weekend something would come up with my friends, and I'd ask Amy for a rain check, until she finally said, "I'm totally disillusioned with you. Don't bother coming. You're nothing but a selfish capitalist."

Wrong. It wasn't true. I wanted to see her and meet her friends as much as she wanted me to, but I just didn't have the time. So, to try to win back her confidence, I sent her group another thousand-dollar check.

Sheila was right in what she'd said the night we went out to dinner. I *was* busier than when I'd been working. It was hard being a millionaire. I called Lynne often to read her my fund letters: *Dear Mike, My mom won't buy me a dog. Will you buy me one?* But we still hadn't answered any. The three boxes of mail were overflowing by now. Something had to be done.

So anyway, my life was more hectic but a lot more interesting than it had been. There were a few little inconveniences, like trying to keep my checkbook straight. Lennie Thompson was still leaving messages, and that same car seemed to be cruising our house sometimes. Another hitch. I wasn't drawing as much as I wanted to. How could I, with my creativity going into thinking up ways to spend money?

Unlimited possibilities!—that's what I had now. More than seventy-four thousand dollars in my account at the moment and another ninety-four thousand dollars every year for nineteen more years. I'd probably go with Mercer's safe investments eventually, but what was the big rush? Having that money where I could get it gave me a huge sense of power.

Power. Oh, man. I guess everybody wants it. During this period, things had been pretty peaceful between my father and me. He was out most of the time, showing clients those bum properties without anybody taking a bite. But on this one night in March the powder keg blew up.

I had failed a quiz that day, and Chu got on the telephone. When my dad heard the news, it was as if something snapped. CRRR-AAACK!

"It was one little quiz!" I argued.

"You're staying in every night until you have an A plus!"

I had planned to meet the guys at seven. "You mean you're grounding me?" I laughed.

His eyebrows shot up. "What's the matter, you think you're *beyond* doing what I tell you to do?"

See what I mean about power? I'll spare the details of how my mom tried unsuccessfully to get us to calm down. I couldn't see staying in, when my math was actually done for the next day. My dad didn't care if it was done or not, which proves he was only throwing his weight around. "You're studying tonight," he said. I hated to buck him, but this was ridiculous. "I've got an appointment," I finally told him, and I walked out of the house.

I drove over to Freddy's News, where we had planned to meet, and waited for Barry, Ron, and Lingo. I felt bad about my dad, but hell, I was eighteen years old. Old enough to run my own life, and financially independent. He had a lot of nerve to be grounding me. "Where to?" I asked the guys when they piled into my car.

"Bowling?" Lingo suggested.

"*Bor*-ing!"

"How about going into the city?" Ron asked us. "There's this new club called Vision. They've got a forty-foot-in-diameter eyeball that glows in the dark. . . ."

Barry shook his head. "It'll be dead there during the week."

I suddenly got an idea. "Let's make this a night to remember. Let's go down to Atlantic City, to a casino."

"It's over two hours each way," Ron reminded me.

"Time passes quickly in a Camaro."

"Will they let us in?" he asked.

"Maybe not you," Barry mocked him. "They'll take one look at that pathetic mustache of yours and say, 'No teen-agers allowed, sonny.'"

"How old are you supposed to be to get in?"

"Twenty-one, but we can pass. Let's go," I decided. "Just let me run in Freddy's for a second and get a pack of gum."

Freddy's News seemed to be empty when I went in, except for Martin, Freddy's nephew who works there. "Hey, Moneybags, how's it going?" he yelled, slapping my palm.

"Great. A pack of gum, please."

"Only gum? Come on, spend!" He pushed a display card at me. "How about some gold pens, some solid silver razor blades? Nothing's too good for Mike Bronti."

"Okay, give me the works," I said throwing down a twenty and taking some blades off the display card.

"What are you up to these days?" Marty gave me my change.

"Going down to Atlantic City."

"Tonight?"

"Yeah, my friends are waiting for me. They're out in my car."

"That red Camaro is yours?"

"Yeah."

"Nice. Well, good luck," Martin said, "as if *you* needed luck!"

At that point I heard a croaky voice from the booth in the back mumble, "Bronti?"

Oh, no—*Thompson*, all alone, reading the *National Enquirer* or some other rag. I tried to duck out, but he caught me before I could reach the door. What a weirdo. Skinny like a giraffe. Was he high or something? I wondered. Anyway, his eyes were kind of squinty, maybe just from reading in the dim light.

"Where's my share, Bronti?" he asked, coming close enough to breathe in my face. "You owe me. That was *my* ticket. Tonight is the night."

"Get out of my life, Thompson," I said.

He shoved the newspaper at me, so that I thought he was trying to hit me, but then he said, "Look at my horoscope. See what it says? *'Evening hours important. You will get what you've been waiting for tonight.'*"

I pulled a couple of coins from my pocket. "Okay, you've been waiting and now you're getting it. Eighty-five cents!" I slapped the coins in his palm. "Now we're even, good night!"

"Hey!" Thompson shouted.

"He's off the wall," Martin mouthed to me as I pushed past Thompson and went out. I glanced over my shoulder, but Thompson wasn't following me.

"What took you so long?" the guys wanted to know when I was back in the car again.

As I pulled away from the curb, I filled them in on what had happened inside.

"Should've gone in there with you," Lingo said gruffly.

"Unnecessary," Ron snorted. "Thompson's stupid but harmless. His brain's smaller than his Adam's apple. He's a *dropout*, what do you expect from him? Whoops, sorry, Barry, no offense!"

14

The two-hour drive went pretty quickly. We spent the time gabbing. We were talking about how the four of us had gotten to be friends in the first place. "It's totally logical," Ron said to Barry and Lingo. "Mike and I tripped over you two crude lumps of protoplasm and figured that under our superior-influence you might make it as human beings."

"Wrong." Barry, in the back, banged his knees against the front seat. "I asked myself, who are the three guys who most need me to lead them out of Disneyland into the real world?"

"No, *this* is it." I glanced at Barry in the rearview mirror. "Barry psyched out which three guys he knew were most likely to strike it rich, and he's playing up to us so that someday we'll be his customers!"

"Nah, I don't need you guys," Barry said, lighting a cigarette and blowing smoke through his nose. "I've got a whole list of potential customers just from making telephone calls. Of course, if one of you *wanted* to buy at Glenhaven Commons, I could get you a special price.

Sean, my boss, is making it easy for young people to buy in. He thinks it's unfair that some developers discriminate against young people."

After we'd been driving down the parkway for maybe half an hour, Lingo interrupted whoever was talking and said, "Mike, see that car?"

"Where?"

"Right behind us. It's been tailgating for a while."

"Go faster," Barry suggested. "See if they're playing games or what."

I floored the pedal. I was curious anyway to see what the Camaro could do on the open road. "There, did I lose it?"

Lingo nodded. "No way an old Plymouth could keep up with *this*, man."

"Huh?" An old Plymouth was the kind of car that had been cruising my house. I looked in the mirror but I couldn't see it now. Was somebody following me or something? Lingo was right, though, no old Plymouth could keep up with us.

Then for a while, to pass the time, we played a dumb name game, where one of us gave the initials of a rich person. "J.P.G.," I said.

"Living or dead?" the guys asked me, and they finally guessed J. Paul Getty, who had made a lot of money in oil and gas and stuff.

"H.H."

"Howard Hughes!"

"K.M.," Lingo said.

We tried to guess for a while, and then we finally wanted to give up, but Lingo wouldn't tell us. He wanted us to keep guessing. Anyway, at that point we had better things to think about. We were coming into Atlantic City.

"Hey, which casino do you want to go to? " I asked as we left the parkway.

"The Golden Fleece," Barry said. "It's definitely the best."

I followed the signs to the Golden Fleece as we drove from the parkway. It was almost ten o'clock by now, but the town looked wide awake. Not like Glenfield, where even the movie closes down on week nights. I pulled into the Golden Fleece's parking lot and turned my car over to an attendant.

"Seriously," Barry warned us just before we entered the casino, "act mature, okay? They've got plainclothes guards circulating, looking for underage guys. Act cool. No schoolboy stuff or horsing around if you happen to win a few bucks. Well, this is it. What do you think?"

The other three of us stood and stared. It was our first time in a casino, after a sheltered life in Glenfield, where the only gambling is the wheel of chance at the Mercy Hospital Bazaar. So picture our eyes going *boing, boing* at the sight of huge marble columns, red velvet walls, mirrored ceilings, and blinking baseboard lights. Waitresses in tiny little skirts were serving drinks on big trays, and the croupiers, who run the games, were all dressed in black tuxedos. There was real music in the background, but the sounds I liked best were the *clickety-click* of the wheel of fortune and the *clunk* and *whirr* of the slot machines.

The place was crowded with all kinds of people—from a few other people who looked as young as we were, all the way up to senior citizens who were standing in line behind the nickel slot machines. There were men bent over their cards, muttering curses under their breath, and gorgeous women tossing bills to croupiers and then scooping up their chips.

"See anybody who might be a plainclothesman?" I whispered to Barry.

He studied faces. "No, not at the moment. I think we're okay."

"So let's get started." I took out my wallet. "Here, you guys, this is on me. I would've liked to give you more, but I didn't know we were coming and this is all the cash I've got—a hundred bucks each."

Barry led us to the cashier's booth, where we exchanged our paper money for chips and quarters. "I suggest we split up," Barry said, "so we don't look like four bimbo kids."

He went off by himself then, toward the twenty-one table, and for the moment I envied him. Barry knew his way around. I didn't even know how to play twenty-one, and there was Barry, looking so confident. I'd have to start learning some things from him, maybe even a few things about real estate.

"Okay, I'm starting," I said to Ron and Lingo, and I headed for a slot machine. When both of them followed me, I didn't object. It wouldn't be any fun alone. The three of us watched while a woman in a tight dress, with lots of makeup, began feeding silver dollars into two machines at once. "Here, honey," she winked at me, "play one for me." She handed me a coin. I put it in, pulled the arm, and a gush of silver dollars poured out. "Yahooo!"

"Bronti's got the touch!" Lingo shouted. "This guy's unbeatable!"

"Oh, honey, you're so *good*! Go again!" the woman called.

We helped her collect her silver dollars—there were only about twenty—and although she wanted me to keep playing them, I sensed it was time to move on. Barry was right; we might attract attention, especially if we hung around with—whoever she was. I thought about how Sheila was jealous, and I motioned to the guys. "Come on. Barry's probably looking for us. Good luck," I said to the woman. "Maybe we'll see you later. So long!"

"Oh, come on and stay, boys!" she said, looking sad as we left.

I led Ron and Lingo across the casino, where we pretended to be searching for Barry. Soon we stopped, though, at a roulette table, and Ron said, "Come on, let's try this. Why not?" All three of us put down chips—Ron and I a whole pile each, Lingo one at a time—and then we watched the ball whirl in the spinning bowl, hoping it would stop at the number we picked. No luck.

After we had lost most of our money at roulette, we went up to the second level. From there we could look down and see everything that was going on below. We saw Barry talking to a good-looking woman.

"What do you think he's saying to her?" Lingo asked me.

"He's probably selling her a townhouse," I said sarcastically, but the truth was, I was envious. I hadn't even answered any of the come-on letters from women I'd been getting, because I didn't know what to *say*, like Barry did.

What a scene—neon lights, bubbling fountain, people laughing. And then I noticed someone watching me. A guy in his early twenties, maybe, with wavy reddish hair. A plainclothes guard, I was sure of it. He seemed to be glancing at Ron and at Lingo, too. I nudged them. "Let's move."

We went downstairs again, to the wheels of fortune which I remembered from Mercy Hospital, except that there you won stuffed animals and here you could win big bucks. I looked over my shoulder while I was playing the few chips I had left. Was the plainclothesman still watching me? I thought I saw someone with red hair on the stairs, coming down.

GOLDEN FLEECE SIFTS OUT MINORS. UNDERAGE MILLIONAIRE NABBED IN CASINO . . . Ron and Lingo didn't seem to notice anything, but I was certain we were going to be caught. "Somebody's following us!" I nudged them, leading them to a table where men and women were seated on stools. The redheaded guy was on us, I could have sworn it! I crouched down quickly, as if I had dropped something under the table.

"What are you doing?" a woman cried as I brushed against her leg.

"Oh, excuse me!" I popped up again. "Nothing—I'm sorry, nothing! Let's get out of here," I hissed at Ron and Lingo. "Somebody's about to ask for our ID!"

They didn't believe me, they said I was paranoid as we took the long way around to the slot machines. I had to admit once we were there that I didn't see the plainclothesman at all. We did see Barry, though, waving and smiling. "How'd you make out?" Lingo asked him.

"Cleaned out, as far as money goes, but I met a twenty-seven-year-old woman who thinks I'm twenty-eight. How did you guys do?"

"I'm wiped out," Ronnie told him.

Lingo and I began emptying the remaining quarters out of our pockets.

"There's still a chance," Lingo said hopefully. He dropped his coins in the machine until the last one disappeared, and he let out a moan.

"You going to play yours?" Barry asked me.

"Sure." I rubbed my hands together, stepped up, and dropped four quarters in the nearest slot machine, and then four more after that, until I was down to my last four. "So—easy come, easy go," I said, plunking them sloppily in the slot. Barry yawned and walked away, but Lingo and Ronnie hung in. I pulled the arm and let go, expecting the *whirr, click*, and silence. Instead, three lemons ended up in a line, and a stream of quarters gushed out! *Yiiiyiiiyee!*

I drew a cartoon of it later—coins spilling out like a waterfall. It took me more by surprise, in a way, than the lottery win. I didn't hit the jackpot—too bad—but I won back my four hundred dollars. GOLDEN LOTTERY WINNER CONTINUES ON A ROLL!

Ron, Lingo, and Barry ran around finding Styrofoam cups to collect my money in while I stood almost ankle deep in it and a bunch of people started to gather around.

"Play again, Mike." Lingo scooped up quarters. "This guy can't lose," he announced to the onlookers. "He won the Pick-Six Lottery a couple of weeks ago. He's putting Glenfield on the map."

"No kidding, you won the lottery?" people in the group started asking me. "Keep playing!" they urged me. "Go on, keep it going!"

I gave the machine four more quarters while the guys were still picking up my winnings, but after that I felt funny. I was attracting too much attention. When all the coins were in the cups, I motioned for the guys to come with me, and we carried the quarters to the cashier to exchange for paper money.

"You remind me of K.M.," Lingo said as we waited for our turn.

"Who's K.M.?" Barry thumped him. "Come on, Linganelli—we give up!"

"King Midas."

"King isn't a first name!" Barry moaned. "You're so simpleminded, Linganelli. I bet you think Midas got rich selling mufflers. Come on, you *do*. Admit it!"

"No, I don't!" Lingo blushed.

Ron tapped my shoulder when it was my turn with the cashier. "Keep one cupful of change for luck, for the next time you come."

"Okay, you hold on to it." I took the bills from the cashier and put them in my wallet. "I'll be back in a minute, you guys, I have to go to the john."

"Me, too," Lingo said, shadowing me as usual.

"Okay, we'll meet you there." I pointed out a spot to Ronnie and Barry. And then Lingo and I went out of the casino and looked for a men's room in the Golden Fleece Hotel. "Next time we'll stay over," I told him, glancing up at the gold fixtures. "Celebrity suite, room service, we'll have the whole bit."

"That'd be good," Lingo agreed. "Hey," he said, "there's the can."

We went in. Fancy bathroom. I finished quicker than he did and said to him, "Take your time, man. I'll wait for you outside in the hall." I had no sooner stepped out than who should come up and shake hands with me but the redheaded guy.

"Hi, Mike," he patted my arm, "how're you doing?"

"Fine." Ah, so he *knew* me. "Tell me your name," I said. "I forget."

"From Glenfield—?"

"Yeah? Have I met you?"

"Guess who else is here from Glenfield?"

"Who?"

He smiled and took me by the arm. "Somebody who really wants to see you. Come say hello."

This is the price you pay for fame, I was thinking as I followed him. "Funny, " I started to tell him, "know who I thought you were?"

Instead of answering, he steered me around the corner into an alcove, where I remember seeing an ice machine. At that point whatever happened—I'm not very clear. Someone tall, his face covered with a stocking, leaped out, and the two of them jumped me. My knees buckled, I went down, and my face hit the floor.

15

Picture a guy flat on his face with birds tweeting around his head. *Me.* I could actually see why comic-book artists showed unconscious people that way. If I was out cold, it was just for a second, but there was a birdlike sound in my ears as I scuffled with the two guys while they pinned me down, grabbed my wallet, jumped up, and ran away. Bastards! The next thing I knew, Lingo was bending over me, saying, "Holy hell, what *happened* to you?"

"Get those guys!" I mumbled.

"Who?"

"They ripped off my wallet!" I tried to get up.

"Take it easy." He helped me. "*Who?* Hey, your nose is bleeding. What *happened?* Man, you're *bleeding!*" He felt for a tissue, and when he couldn't find one, he pulled off his outer shirt. "Here!"

I shook my head. "I don't need it." I wiped my nose with my hand. "It's only a little blood. Let's get those guys before they get away!"

"Who?" Lingo asked me. "Tell me what *happened.* Which way'd they go?"

Leaning on Lingo and catching my breath, I looked down both corridors. Which way? I wasn't sure. *Tweet, tweet,* I was still hearing birds.

Lingo insisted on mopping my nose with his shirt. "Look, let me take you to Ron and Barry. Come on." He blinked at the sight of blood. "Then I'll go out looking by myself."

"I want to go with you!" I tried to pull free of him, but he practically dragged me back to the casino, while all the time I kept muttering, "Let me go with you, come on!"

"What'd they look like?" Lingo asked me as we reentered the casino.

"Did you see that bozo watching me before? Red hair, I thought he was a guard. . . . The other guy had a stocking over his face. . . . *How come you aren't helping me find them?* I thought you were such an amazingly hotshot bodyguard, man!"

"Calm down." Lingo wiped my nose again as we spotted Ron and Barry. "You shouldn't be running around chasing muggers. Stay here and cool down. I'll go back and check out the john and the hall where we were walking. . . ."

Ron and Barry, coming up to us, took one look at me. "What *happened*?"

"Some muggers jumped me and took my wallet when I came out of the john!"

"Who? What? Where?" They started in, as if they were bucking for reporter on the *Independent.* The only story *I* was interested in was BRONTI BRAVES BRUTAL BEATING, SEEKS AND FINDS FEARSOME FOES.

"Somebody mugged you?" Ron was furious. "What are we waiting for, let's report it."

"No, they could hassle us," Barry argued. "We're not supposed to be here. Let's cut our losses and beat it. Too bad about the bucks, but at least you're all in one piece—"

"I'm looking for them," I said.

"*I'll* go," Lingo offered.

Ron saw I wasn't taking no for an answer. "If one of us goes, we *all* will."

So I described the guy with red hair and we all went back to the scene of the crime.

No luck. The corridors were empty. No sign of the redhead in the bathroom. Eventually we came back into the casino and wandered from game to game. After a half hour it was clear: "They could have left and be home in bed by now," Ronnie said. Even I agreed there was nothing to do but get my car and go home.

"Want me to drive?" Barry asked.

I touched my face very cautiously and then climbed into the backseat. The guys knew if I was letting Barry drive, I must be feeling really bad.

On the way home we forgot about the fun of the evening and talked only about the mugging. We'd been driving for an hour when Barry suddenly said, out of the blue, "I know who the guy wearing the stocking over his face must've been."

"Who?"

He glanced over his shoulder at me. "Loony Lennie Thompson."

Now Ron and Lingo looked at me. "Well, *could* it have been?"

"What makes you think that?" I asked Barry.

"He's been wanting money from you, right? Did he know you were coming here?"

"I told Martin tonight . . ."

"And Thompson was right there listening."

"Yeah, I guess, but—"

"Thompson doesn't have a car, does he?" Ron interrupted.

"He could have a friend with a *Plymouth*," Lingo said. "That car that was tailgating us—"

"You think"— I paused, trying to figure it out—"you think—wait—the guy with red hair was a friend of Lennie Thompson's? Glenfield! He mentioned Glenfield. 'Somebody wants to see you,' he said. He meant Thompson! And back at Freddy's, Thompson's horoscope—'*You're going to get what you want tonight*,' or whatever . . ."

"He got what he wanted, all right," Lingo muttered. "Who's the redheaded friend? I think I've seen him around Freddy's."

"We thought we'd lost that Plymouth on the parkway," Ron went on. "They probably dropped back on purpose. Then they caught up and followed us to the casino, and watched—"

"Until Mike was alone," Barry said. "How much money did they get from you?"

"The four hundred I won from the slots. But the point isn't the *money*."

"Naturally," Ronnie said. "How does your face feel?"

It was killing me. "Okay, it's okay."

We were quiet a few seconds. "Loony Thompson," Ronnie muttered.

"Well," Lingo said, "at least now we *know*."

Knowing, as it turned out, gave us a wave of new energy. The three of them wasted it by talking. I stored mine silently inside.

"Maybe we'll pass them on the way." Barry stepped up his speed again.

"Forget it." Ronnie shook his head. "They probably had a big head start."

"Is Thompson a retard or what?" Lingo asked. "No, wait, I'm not kidding. I heard he's mental."

"He's into horoscopes," I snorted.

"He reminds me of a giraffe," Ronnie said.

Lingo shifted his weight so that the whole backseat quivered. "We can't let him get away with this. Let me take care of him, okay?"

"*I'm* taking care of him," I said, but they were too wrapped up in themselves to hear.

"Report him to the Glenfield police," Ronnie was saying. "Tell them how he's been phoning you all the time."

"Forget the cops," Lingo told me. "I'll take care of Thompson tomorrow after school. I'll find out where he lives and make him swallow his Adam's apple."

Barry slowed down for a tollbooth, where we had to dip into my one remaining cupful of quarters. "How about bugging *him* with phone calls, like he did to you?"

I let them blab on about what I should do. Each one of them thought he had the answer. Meanwhile I pretended to be falling asleep, so I could think to myself. The guys meant well, but this was something *I* had to handle. Thompson had set *me* up, not them. It was going to be up to me to get revenge on my own.

When we hit Glenfield at almost five A.M., Barry drove Ronnie and Lingo home first. "Want my dad to speak to his friend who's a detective?" Ronnie asked as he got out of the car.

"No," I said, irritated. "I'll take care of it."

"You guys aren't going to school, are you?" Lingo asked.

"I've got to," Ron said. "I've got a test."

"Are you going?" Lingo asked me.

I stalled. "I don't know."

Lingo got out of the car. "I'll find you after I get some sleep, either at school or I'll call you at home. Now, don't worry about Thompson. *I'll* handle him, no sweat."

I didn't argue. What the heck, let him think it was okay with me.

"So long, Mike, see you in school," Ron said.

"I'm not leaving you out of sight from now on!" Lingo called. "Good night!"

As Barry and I headed toward Freddy's so Barry could get his car, rain started to fall and it began to get light. "Don't get physical with Thompson," Barry advised me. "Come over to my place later on and I'll help you think up something smart."

Again I didn't say anything except "Yeah, okay. So long."

After Barry had taken off, I got behind the wheel of my car. Seeing myself in the mirror, I knew I couldn't go to school or straight home. I was half asleep, my eyelids were swollen, there was dried blood on my nose. Anyway, this was the time to go after Thompson, while I was as angry as I was now.

Where to find him, though, at this hour, not even six in the morning. Freddy's was open already, so I decided to go in. Maybe Thompson would be in there. Nah, that was expecting a miracle. But Freddy might know where Thompson lived, which would at least set me on the right path.

"What's the matter, rich men can't sleep good?" Freddy asked when he saw me.

"I don't need much sleep," I told him. "I've got too much to do. Martin's not here?"

"No, he worked late and he's home sleeping. Hey, you don't look so good . . ."

"I bumped into an ice machine," I told him. "Cup of coffee, please." I was determined to stay awake. Too bad Martin wasn't available—he might have overheard Lennie saying he was going to get me last night.

Freddy poured me my coffee. "Some pretty tough ice machine. Where do they have bruisers like that?"

"Down in Atlantic City," I said.

"Looks like you fought a one-armed bandit and lost. You got to watch yourself in A. City."

I nodded and cleared my throat. "When did you see Lennie Thompson last?" I asked him.

"Yesterday." Freddy shoved milk and sugar across the counter. "He's driving me nuts. He reads his horoscope without buying the paper, and when he puts it back, it's a mess, so nobody'll buy it. The guy's got a screw loose."

"I know." I paused. "Martin's asleep you say? I couldn't call him?"

Freddy shook his head. "Forget it. He'd kill you for waking him. What's the problem?"

"Just something—personal." I drank my coffee. It had to be Thompson, *had* to be. "Have you ever seen Thompson in here with a redheaded guy?" I asked.

"He's usually alone," Freddy said. "He gets a lift home once in a while."

"In an old Plymouth?"

"A Plymouth?" Freddy scratched his chin. "Plymouth? Could be."

Damn it, *get* Thompson, I told myself, before he strikes a

second blow. "You happen to know where Thompson lives?" I asked, trying to sound cool.

"No, can't say I do."

North Glenfield, I remembered. He had mentioned it once on the telephone. As Freddy turned back to his work, I flipped through his phone book. Thompson would probably be home sleeping. I'd rout him out of bed and clobber him. Damn, *two* pages of Thompsons but no listing under Lennie. I scanned the street names. Hallelujah, only two Thompsons in North Glenfield. I jotted down the addresses. "So long, Freddy," I said, reaching for money to pay. And then remembered. "I got wiped out in Atlantic City. Can I owe you for the coffee?"

"You got free coffee for life, as long as I'm behind this counter, Mike. But for your own good," he sounded like my father, "*watch* yourself in Atlantic City. They got all kinds of scum and lowlifes down there."

"I know," I said as I left, raring to go now, "almost as low and scummy as we've got here in Glenfield!"

16

I got into my car and roared away from the curb. It was raining now, harder. Tired as I was, heading toward North Glenfield, I got a second wind. The bridge of my nose began to throb, which made me feel even angrier than before, and the bitter coffee taste in my mouth made me feel mean. The nerve of Thompson, jumping me. His stupid phone messages I could handle, but did he seriously think I'd let him get away with beating me up? Big headlines flashed before my eyes—LOTTERY CHAMP SQUASHES LOONY MUGGER, HOROSCOPE NUT SEES STARS! I was already looking forward to telling the guys how I'd done it all by myself.

I turned off Main at Adams Boulevard, where there was a sign that said NORTH GLENFIELD. The road was depressing, with stores and factories lined up on both sides. The first address on my list was 140 Farber, which I was pretty sure was a street off Adams that went up a steep hill. I slowed down to look at street names—Clancy Street, Durban . . . As soon as I slowed, my car started to sputter.

What the hell . . . ? It was coughing now, sounding awful. Meanwhile I was trying to read street names. Damn, I suddenly noticed the gas gauge was below empty. I'd last put gas in before Atlantic City. So what? No big deal. Adams Boulevard was the service station capital of the U.S. I turned into the first station I came to and asked the attendant to fill it up.

"Credit card or cash?" he asked.

And then I remembered. "I haven't got either one on me. My wallet was stolen last night. Think you could trust me for ten bucks' worth? I'm going to the bank as soon as it opens—"

"*What?*"

"I know it sounds fishy, but I have plenty of money. I'm the guy who won the Pick-Six Lottery. Maybe you saw me on—"

The attendant shook his head and laughed in my face. "I thought I'd heard everything, man. Move, will you? This other guy's waiting behind you."

"Give me a break, please?" I begged, but all he did was laugh again. *Save your anger for Thompson,* I told myself. Rolling out of there I figured, damn, I'd better park the car somewhere. I didn't want to go dead in the middle of the boulevard. It's *good* this happened, I thought. I was really up for a fight now. Wait till I got my hands on Lennie the Punk.

I drove down Adams, the Camaro gasping, and pulled in at the next greasy-spoon fast-food place. The smell reminded me of Beefarama and stirred up hunger pangs. If I'd had a hundred bucks on me, I'd have given it for one burger. No, better to stay hungry for a while—hungry for revenge. Getting out and locking the car, I asked the first person I saw, "Excuse me, can you tell me where Farber Street is?"

Two streets farther on. I started walking, and when I got there, I darted across the boulevard so that a car screeched and honked. Good, it helped wake me up. The rain was hitting my face and trickling down my neck, but that was good too, I decided. It would keep me alert.

Farber Street—there it was, steep as a ski slope. I'd have paid a fortune right then for a chair lift to take me up. Number—what was it?—140. Let this address be the right one, I prayed. I walked past a shabby little grocery store, with a sign out front that said FREE QUART OF MILK WITH PURCHASE OF $5 BEFORE 7 A.M. By the way, maybe it sounds as if this was routine for me—looking for a fight like this. The fact was, I hadn't had a fight since I was thirteen years old, when someone heard my grandma talking like she does and said, "Your grandma's a wop!" Anyway, this was the first time in years that I was looking for blood.

I kept climbing, huffing and puffing, past a row of gray attached houses. Number 110, 112—what should I do when I got there, ring the bell? What if it was the wrong place? Don't think about it. What if Thompson *answered.* Punch him in the stomach! Flatten him! *Pow! Ffft! Oooofff! Uggh! Iiiieee!*

Sweating and shivering at the same time, I looked up ahead of me. An old woman was coming toward me, and I lowered my eyes. Ask, maybe, if she knew Lennie? No, keep this anonymous. A man came out of number 130, and I didn't answer when he said hello.

There it was—140, gray like all the other houses, with a long flight of steps leading up to a sagging porch. I had hoped I'd see the Plymouth, but I didn't—not that that proved anything. Catch your breath, I told myself, meanwhile counting the steps—twelve. I started up and then came down. What if this wasn't the right place?

It wasn't. Suddenly I was sure. I crouched behind the steps, which were open underneath, so that I could hide there and look out through a crack. This was ridiculous. What made me think I could pick the right house on my first try? Another person was coming up the hill, so I ducked. By now I was freezing, my hair was wet, and my sleepless night was catching up with me. There was a pounding between my eyes that kept me from seeing straight.

Trying to focus my eyes, I inched out from under the porch steps. I was thinking, I'll wait till this next guy passes and then I'll go, this is dumb. When I looked a second time at the guy, though, sparks of anger burst into flame—tall, skinny, carrying a brown bag, giraffe neck—it was Thompson. What a break! He was by himself! I ducked down again.

In that minute my brain spun like an Atlantic City wheel of fortune. Maybe he'd smash my face a second time. Should I forget revenge? Hell no! Now he was close enough so I could see his Adam's apple. Jamming my hand in my jacket pocket, I touched—razor blades! The ones from Freddy's! Perfect, I thought crazily, give Thompson the scare of his life!

My fingers tore at the wrapping, but Thompson was *here*, and I dropped the blades. Crouched down, I knew he couldn't see me, especially with the rain in his face. I took a flying leap and tackled him so that we toppled to the sidewalk together, and Thompson's bag hit the sidewalk with a *splat!* and a *crack!*

It was a cinch, a total victory. Thompson had no idea what was happening. I pinned him as easily as I used to pin Amy when we were eight and ten years old. Sitting on his stomach, I held his arms and thrust my face close to his. Amazing how light he was, how puny. I watched his Adam's apple twitch. "Not much fun, is it?" I spat out. A gust of wind whipped our faces. "What did you do with my wallet?" He wasn't hurt bad, I was sure, but he looked terrified.

"Wallet?" he croaked. "I don't have nothing in my wallet. Just don't take my chain, okay?"

"Take your chain?" I bellowed. "I'm not mugging you, you mugged *me*, you jerk!"

He squinted as if he was just now recognizing me. "Bronti? What—? What's—?"

I glanced down at the chain he was so worried about—a gold thing with a horoscope charm on it that looked to me as if it was turning his neck green. Pressing my thumbs into his weak biceps, I fired questions like bullets. "You gonna deny following me down to Atlantic City? Who's your redheaded friend who set me up? Whose Plymouth, huh? Huh? And where're my credit cards?"

Thompson gasped and blinked in confusion. "You're an Aquarius. I shoulda known, Aquariuses are always beating on me. . . . I haven't done nothing to you but ask you for what the horoscope said I was gonna get. . . ." He suddenly wrenched his shoulders frantically and raised his head up a little. "Hey, where's my stuff from the market?"

I looked next to us on the sidewalk. His bag had split down the middle. A carton had broken open and a trickle of milk was running out.

"Please," he said, almost crying, "she's waiting for it. We're outta cash. She'll *kill* me if it's ruined—"

"Admit it!" I squeezed his wrists now. "Admit you and your buddy followed me down to Atlantic City!"

"What buddy?" Thompson whimpered. "I never been down there in my *life*!"

He could have been acting, faking me out, but—no, this weakling wasn't the guy with the stocking mask. "Where were you then, last night after Freddy's?" I pumped him, easing up on my grip.

"I stayed there till they closed," he said, straining toward the split bag. "Ask Martin." He wrenched again. "Please let me up!"

"I'm checking your story with Martin!" I talked tough, but the hot angry streak had gone out of me. I slid off Thompson's puny chest and helped the guy up.

"Oh, no," he wailed as he got a good look at the damage. A carton of eggs had broken open and yolks were dripping.

Just then the door of 140 opened. "What's going on, Lennie?" a woman asked.

His mother? His grandmother? Whoever it was, her voice sounded strained.

"Hey, please," Thompson begged me, "split before she comes out here. My mom'll think *I* started something. She always thinks that!"

I picked up the torn, wet bag and handed it to him. *The guy was afraid of his own mother.* Without saying anything else, I did what he wanted and quickly took off.

I felt pretty lousy as I tripped over my own feet running down Farber Street. *Grr! Thwack! Arrrgh! Oooof!*—all over the wrong guy. Somewhere the right guys—strangers, probably, who'd overheard in the casino that I was the lottery winner from Glenfield—were sleeping and dreaming of what they'd buy with my cash and credit cards. Whatever meanness I should have saved for them, I had just spent on pathetic Lennie. LOTTERY CHAMP, what a laugh. Make that MIKE THE CHUMP.

Now what? I wasn't thinking too well. I wandered back to the Adams Boulevard parking lot. My car was safe, but it wouldn't do me any good until I got money for gas. What time was it? Almost eight. Bank not open yet. Parents would be off to work by now. They wouldn't be there to see me, so hitching a ride on a bakery truck, I went home and fell into bed.

17

Sleeping in the daytime is weird. I had a lot of bad dreams. In one of them, Lennie Thompson told me his mom had died, and I woke up thinking maybe it was true. All I could picture, as I lay there, was milk trickling down the sidewalk and Lennie's mom trying to collect it and not being able to. About three in the afternoon, I opened my eyes and saw my own mom standing beside my bed.

"Mike, you're *here*!"

"Yeah." I sat up, dazed.

"Where *were* you? Why didn't you call us?" She bent over me, touching my chin. "What in the world *happened* to you? Why didn't you call us? What's wrong with your eyes?"

"My eyes?" My *nose* was what hurt. "Somebody mugged me, but I'm okay," I mumbled. "They got my wallet, that's all."

"Who? When? Where did this happen?" She sat down on the bed, looking shaken. "Why didn't you get in touch with us? From three in the morning on, we kept trying to call your friends. Couldn't you get to a phone somehow?

We were sure something terrible had happened. We even called the police!"

"What for?" I moaned. All I needed at this point was the police on my back. "I would have called, but it was late and I didn't want to wake you up."

"I'm awake *anyway* when you're out all night." She rocked the bed so hard that Muttsy came out from under it. "So explain this to me. Where *were* you?"

"In Atlantic City."

"Atlantic City! How did you end up *there*? And who did that to you? Your eyes—!"

"Two guys jumped me."

"Who?"

"I don't know. I thought I knew, but—" I decided not to go into the Lennie Thompson story. "It's nothing serious, anyway."

"Nothing serious! Look!" She handed me a mirror.

Oh, man. The Technicolor had come out while I was sleeping—I had two huge purplish-black half circles under my eyes. "It looks worse than it is," I said, sinking down in bed again.

My mom shooed Muttsy off the bed, as if I was too fragile or something. "What were you doing in Atlantic City in the first place?"

"I took Ronnie and the guys down, just to have some fun, you know? I won some money, and then I got mugged. Coming out of the bathroom—two guys pulled me down. Strangers, I'm pretty sure. Maybe they recognized me from the lottery ad."

"Grandma's been afraid of that all along! Does it hurt much?" my mom asked. "Oh, Mike! We were frantic! Do you think your nose is broken?"

Why couldn't she just let me rest? "Nah, don't worry about it," I said. "My nose'll be okay."

"I can't understand why you didn't—I called up Ron's and Joe's parents in the middle of the night and woke them. They were worried too! Are Ron and Joe home now?"

"Yeah, I guess."

"You don't know?"

"Yeah, they're home!" My head was pounding.

"What are you angry about? *We're* the ones who should be angry, after you were so rude to Dad and then didn't come home all night. He felt terrible because of your argument. He's out looking for you right now. How long have you been home?"

"All day, I've been sleeping."

"He was here earlier. He must not have looked in your bed. Wait"—she listened—"here he comes." We both heard his car. "I'll go down and tell him you're home. We'll also have to notify the police right away." She shook her head as she left. "Oh, your poor eyes!"

I heard my parents talking downstairs and then telephoning. Okay, so I should have called them, but why were they carrying on like this? Ron's and Lingo's parents, too—they were all much too nervous. Barry DeVane's parents didn't make him call and explain where he was every night.

After my mom had gone down, I took another look in the mirror. If I had been in a better mood, I probably would have laughed. I looked like I needed to put raw steaks on my eyes, like guys with shiners do in comic strips. As it was, all I wanted to do was hide my face.

I had just flopped down on top of the covers again when

I heard my parents coming. Muttsy jumped up on the bed now, as if to give me moral support. My dad's footsteps were slow and heavy. I could have pretended to be asleep, but I doubted they would buy that, so I waited, propped up on my pillow. "Hi," I said as they came in.

"Hi," my dad grunted. Coming over to the bed, he studied my raccoon eyes. My mom was standing there watching me silently, and then the two of them exchanged a look. "You didn't know these—attackers?" he asked.

"No." I cleared my throat. "They must've been . . . Atlantic City lowlifes."

He came closer now and finally said, "Are you hurt anywhere else?"

"No, I'm fine."

"Yeah, real fine. Who were these guys, gangsters or what? How old?"

"My age. A little older, maybe."

For a second he seemed about to soften, but then he said, "I'm going to be wanting a blow-by-blow description of your doings from the time you left here." He turned to my mom. "Make him an appointment with Dr. Munro. We'd better check this thing out."

I glared at him. "Why?"

He looked at me impatiently. "To make sure there's no brain damage." He paused. "The way you've been acting lately, I think there must have been some *before* this thing happened!"

"Louis—"

"What do you mean?" I sat up so quickly that Muttsy let out a yelp.

"I mean, we're glad it wasn't *worse*," my dad said. "That goes without saying. But something's wrong here when your so-called good luck is driving the rest of us nuts!" He shut his eyes for a second and began pacing back and forth by my bed. "Your mother thinks the big problem is that I didn't accept the car from you. For once and for all, let's put that issue to rest. I felt the decision to send the car back was in your best interests as well as mine, and even if you don't see it that way, I don't think that gives you license to ignore our house rules."

"House rules?" I repeated. "What is this, an institution?"

"The family *is* an institution," he said, "*yes!*"

"An institution that protects," my mom explained. "If it didn't, I'd hate to think what life would be like. . . . Mike, we're worried. Sometimes it seems as if the values we've tried to teach you have disappeared since you won the money. I won't say it's the money's fault, so that means the fault must be *ours*."

"*His*," my dad corrected her.

"When things aren't going well in a family," she insisted, "usually everybody's at fault in some way."

My dad stopped in his tracks. "I don't agree. I don't buy this idea that a kid's weaknesses can always be laid on the parents. He's not being responsible. That was his problem before he won the money, and it's still his problem now."

"The money has exaggerated it," my mom said. "He wasn't cutting classes before—were you?"

"No! What's so bad, anyway? I've cut maybe ten classes in all."

"What about today?" my dad shot back.

"Okay, so sixteen, grand total. So what?"

"The problem's much bigger than cutting classes!"

"Why, what else?" My head was killing me. "Tell me, *what else*?"

"Mike, calm down," my mom stepped between us. "If Dad's lost his patience, maybe it's because he also lost *a night's sleep* because of you."

"So what else is wrong with me?" I hollered, a little louder than I meant to.

"*What else?*" My dad's voice shook. "Well, let's start with family. You have all the time in the world for friends, and even strangers, but no time for your sister or consideration for us! You—"

"Mike," my mom interrupted, "you've hurt Amy badly. She wants your *interest* in her, not your money! She mentioned on the phone that she's going to return both your checks."

"That's crazy!" I burst out. "I want to go down there, but how can I do all these things? If she sends back my checks, it'll be just like Dad turning down the car." I faced him now, my nose a balloon. "Whatever I try to do, you and Amy only see the bad side. I swear, I'm going to spend all my money entertaining my friends."

"So what else is new?" my dad said, thrusting his hands in his pockets.

Why couldn't they let me alone? I kept thinking—let me deal with this some other time!

"Phil Mercer asked me today again what you've decided," my dad said, "and I was embarrassed to tell him *nothing*. What's the story, Mike? Cars, dinners out, getting into trouble in Atlantic City—are you determined to keep this up until there's nothing left to invest?"

"Yeah."

"How can I deal with that?" He turned to my mom, his jaw jutting out.

"Maybe we should wait until tomorrow . . ." she suggested.

I nodded but my dad shook his head. "We're settling some things *now*." He folded his arms. "I've had enough of his sarcasm."

I met my dad's eyes. "How come you say something sarcastic and it's supposed to be funny, and then *I* do, and you act like I'm a terrible clod?"

"Because I'm your *father*, that's why. If I'd ever been sarcastic with *my* father, I'd have gotten a kick in the rear end and been booted out of the house. We've been too lenient," he said to my mom. "His having all this money is beside the point. For his own good, it's time we make demands and make sure they're carried out."

"I agree we need some guidelines," my mom said, "but maybe we could wait until you're both—rested."

"What are we waiting for," my dad went on, "until he flunks out of school? Until he gets himself into even worse trouble? Until he completely loses respect for us?"

I yawned.

"He's *bored*," my dad said sharply. "First we lose a night's sleep because of him, then we take an interest in helping him, and he sits there and yawns in our faces."

I stood at that point, mostly to wake up, but also to look my dad in the eye. "I can help myself," I muttered. "In case you didn't notice, I'm an adult."

"I'm not convinced," he said. "Sneaking home, sleeping all day with your clothes and shoes on—" He stared at me. *"I'm not convinced."*

"No? Okay, so I guess I'll have to prove I'm an adult." The buzz of anger inside of me became an alarm now.

"Yes, you *will* prove it, by acting responsible and following the rules of the house!"

"Rules of the house?" I mocked.

"Yes. You'll do what I say as long as you live here."

"What if I don't follow the rules?" I rose up on my toes, to make myself seem taller.

He hesitated, but just for a second. "If you don't, it's very simple—then you'll get out."

"You'll throw me out of my own house?"

"*My* own house," he corrected me.

We were eyeball to eyeball now. My mind raced in spite of my headache. "Well, if *that's* how you feel—" I reached for my checkbook and gym bag.

"Mike, wait—" my mom begged.

"Wait for what? I can afford to live on my own!" Slinging the bag over my shoulder, I walked out of the house.

18

Slamming the front door, I kept moving while I groped for my car keys. My mom's voice was still echoing. *Mike, wait! The way to solve problems is to sit down and talk them out!* I wouldn't have been surprised if she had followed me, but probably my dad convinced her not to. They both probably thought I'd come back if they left me alone.

But this time I wasn't going to. I'd show them I was independent. Unfortunately, there was one problem immediately as I was starting my getaway. Standing at the curb, I stared in panic. Somebody stole my car! And then I remembered. My car, minus gas, was still parked in North Glenfield.

I still had no cash on me. And I wasn't going to give my parents the satisfaction of seeing me slink back home. So, shifting my bag, I started walking. I could stay at a hotel on a credit card. Except that my credit cards were gone too, along with my wallet in Atlantic City. Checks, I still had checks, if I could find someone to cash one for me. As I walked I glanced back, relieved that my parents weren't coming after me. I'm not sure I could have held out if my mom had followed me in her car.

The route I took, I took accidentally—down Court and toward Main Street. First of all, I couldn't think straight, with all those little men beating tom-toms inside my head. Plus, I was so mad at my parents, who would never see me as anything but a dumb kid, that I just hunched along and by sheer chance ended up at Beefarama. Maybe Lynne would be working. . . . Great, there she was by the cash register, and Nevelson didn't seem to be around.

"Mike?" She laughed. "Is that *you*? Don't tell me, let me guess—you're tired of being recognized? You're traveling in disguise!"

"Right." It took me a second to remember how I must look to other people. "I've never meant it more than I do now," I told her. "You're a sight for sore eyes."

"Where did you get your sore eyes?" She steered me toward an out-of-the-way booth.

"Oh, from two guys in Atlantic City. Because the disguise is so real-looking, it cost me four hundred bucks."

"Oh, no, you were robbed, too? Do you have any idea who did it?"

"Not really. I know what one of the muggers looks like. I'm going to draw his face and post it all over New Jersey. So how've *you* been?"

"Busy, but not at the moment. Sit down." She sat across from me. "Is everything else okay?"

"Yeah, well, let's see . . . I got into Cummings Institute."

"Sensational!"

"And . . . you know I bought a car." I cleared my throat. "One other thing—I left home just now."

"Left home?" she repeated. "Did something happen? Just for the night, you mean?"

"No, for good. It's time to be on my own."

"What happened? You're not upset about it?"

"No, I'm glad."

"But aren't your parents upset? Where are you staying?"

"At Barry's," I heard myself answering, "just until I get a place of my own."

"Are you sure you're doing the right thing?" Lynne asked. "Do you want to talk about it or anything?"

"No! You sound like my mother!" I said, getting up to call Barry.

Lynne looked at me worriedly. "There's nothing I can do?"

I thought. "Yeah, you could give me credit on a couple of burgers." I hadn't eaten anything, I realized, since before going to Atlantic City.

While I was making arrangements on the phone with Barry, Lynne rustled up a shake and two Ramaburgers, which I wolfed down like a starving man. Then I thanked her and said I'd call her soon, so we could finally get working on the Bronti Fund.

"Where are the letters?" Lynne asked me.

"Still in my parents' house. I'll sneak in some day when they're at work and load up my car. Speaking of cars, Barry's picking me up in a few minutes. He's going to take me to get my Camaro, where it ran out of gas this morning."

Lynne started to say something and then didn't. "That's great about Cummings." She paused. "Have you been drawing much?"

"No, I haven't had time."

"I hope you will soon. I miss seeing your stuff. Where'll you get your comic material, now that you're not living at home?"

I stood up and put on my jacket. "From out in the free world! My family isn't funny. In fact, nothing's been that funny lately."

"Things are still pretty amusing around *here*," Lynne said with a smile. "Drop in at dinner hour, whenever you want a few laughs."

"I'll keep that in mind. So long."

Barry was waiting for me outside. He drove me to get my car and, after he'd lent me money for gas, I followed him over to his place. "You can stay here as long as you want," he said. To show my appreciation, I took him out to a restaurant that let me pay the bill by check. Afterward we called Ron and Lingo, to invite them to Barry's, but because of the Atlantic City caper, the two of them had been grounded for a week. That's when I knew for sure I'd been smart to leave home.

So Barry and I sat around listening to music and working on a six-pack. Barry made lots of bad jokes about the appearance of my face. I didn't say much about my attack on Thompson—I just left Barry with the impression that I'd won after a big struggle. I didn't bother mentioning that poor old Thompson wasn't even the right guy.

That night was the first of many, sitting around enjoying myself at Barry's. "Stay here as long as you want," he said again. "That folding chair pulls out into a bed." We gabbed with the TV on, watched the late movie, and I slept until noon, a practice I could never get away with living at home. The first Sunday morning Lingo phoned to say my parents had called him.

"What'd you tell them?"

"That you're at Barry's."

"Why'd you say that? Now they'll come over here and bug me, try to make me come home—"

"Sorry," Lingo said sheepishly. "I won't tell them anything from now on. What are you doing today?"

"I'm busy." I didn't feel like seeing him. He was acting as if he was my guardian angel or something. "See you around," I cut him off. "Tell Ron I'm busy too."

What I needed was a new scene, a break from people wanting things from me. It was great, getting up when I chose to and not being nagged about cleaning my room. It was nice to be in hiding, where nobody knew my phone number and where the mail wasn't piling up to remind me what I ought to be doing. Of course, my stay with Barry would be temporary. I would be looking for my own apartment. "Let me show you Glenhaven Commons," Barry buzzed in my ear whenever he got a chance.

"Nah, forget it," I would say, "I don't want to buy any fancy townhouse. I'm only going to be here until graduation. Then I'll be off to California."

One day rolled into another, and I kept staying at Barry's. Every time I thought about apartment hunting, Barry would say, "Don't bother—stay on here." I kept going to school during the day, of course, but after school, instead of hanging out with Ron and Lingo, or even Sheila, I often met Barry on his break and then in the evenings we'd go out. This was freedom and I loved it—poker late at night with Barry's work buddies, pizza at two in the morning, dirty laundry piled up in the corner with nobody to make me bring it down.

My new life made it a little rough to get to school on time in the morning. Whenever I was late, the school secretary would give me a dirty look. She knew my mom, and I was sure she was keeping my parents informed about me. To my surprise, though, my parents didn't come looking for me, either at Barry's or at school.

School was boring. I did just enough work to keep out of trouble. In most of my classes I passed the time thinking about all the great things I would do, starting at the end of June. Ryan, the Monk, was always getting me into discussions about whether rich people or poor people were happier. "I'm telling you first hand," I said to him, "I'm happier being rich!"

One day, when I'd been at Barry's a couple of weeks, Ronnie caught up with me in the hall at school. "Did you get it?" he asked.

"Get what?"

"Your room assignment, the name of your roommate."

"My mail's still going to my parents," I said. "I'll have to go over there and get it."

"Want me to go with you?" Ronnie asked.

"No, thanks, I want to sneak in." The fact was, Ron had been annoying me lately, saying negative things about Barry. What was he, jealous? So stupid. I still considered *him* my best friend.

Thinking about room assignments made me wonder what other mail had come for me. Had Amy written or tried to call me? How many more fund letters had come? Man, I should see Mercer, the accountant—I still hadn't gone back to decide on investments. No hurry though. I wasn't spending that much these days—only about three hundred a week.

So life at Barry's was really fun. I'd never had such complete freedom. Another week passed, and another, until I'd been at Barry's a month. I was very surprised that my parents hadn't even tried to call me. Okay, I'd play it their way. I wanted to stop this nonsense, but I could hold out as long as they could.

One slight problem was that living at Barry's wasn't helping my relationship with Sheila. Sheila's parents wouldn't let her visit me there, and she refused to come on the sly. At her house we had no privacy. Whenever I went there, her parents made a fuss over me, which was nice at first but got to be a pain. Before my win, they had just said hello when I came over. Now they were entertaining me and offering me snacks, lunch, and dinner. What was going on, did they want something from me or what?

Okay—guess I'll admit it—there were some other things wrong with living at Barry's. He talked my ear off all the time and was always so sure he was right. He sat around smoking and blowing smoke in my face. He was always sneaking admiring looks at himself in the mirror. But how could I criticize him? The apartment was his, but he was treating me as if it were mine, too.

Anyway, most of the time Barry was great company, always game for some new escapade. For instance, on this one Friday night in early April he suggested that we—I'm embarrassed to be telling this. That we should *get ourselves initiated*, as he put it. Into what? He meant with *women*. Frankly, I was surprised that Barry wasn't already initiated. Still, when he asked me to come with him, I couldn't tell him no. I didn't want to look like a scared kid, so I said, "Okay, sure."

I may as well say at the start that things didn't work out the way we expected them to. Barry knew of a certain street in North Glenfield where women supposedly walked up and down. So we went. I was driving. It was cold and there were snow flurries. My hands were shaking and so icy I figured no woman would let me near her.

"What's the matter?" Barry was mocking me. "Do your teeth chatter when you get horny?"

I bit hard to make them stop chattering. Sheila would *die* if she saw me now. We drove up and down the famous street, but there was no sign of any women available. We considered going into a sleazy place called the Red Beam Bar, but there was a gorillalike bouncer out front. "Let's go home," Barry finally said, and I pretended to be disappointed, but in fact I was relieved.

"Okay, if you want to," I said. "Maybe we'll have better luck another time."

We drove back to the apartment in silence, and I pulled into the lot. All of a sudden, as I parked, I noticed a familiar-looking car. An old Plymouth. The same one I'd seen all those times, including on the way to Atlantic City. "Barry"—I nudged him—"there's that Plymouth! And somebody's in it!" We both got out, sneaked up on the car, and looked in the window. Who was it, the redhaired mugger and his masked partner from Atlantic City? No. Fast asleep, as if she were Goldilocks and we were two of the Three Bears, it was just my number-one fan, pink-haired Mandy Calise.

19

"Barry, is she okay?" I asked, panicked. Mandy didn't seem to be moving. Maybe she couldn't take rejection from me any longer and had come here to end it all. Please, no—not that. I knocked on the window and Mandy sat up, like a zombie.

She screamed when she saw me, as if I were Jack the Ripper instead of her idol.

Her car doors were locked. "Open up," I said, and she finally did when she recognized me.

Covering her face with her hands, she said, "I'm so embarrassed you caught me!"

"You've been following me around like this for a long time, haven't you?"

She nodded.

"Did you follow us to Atlantic City?" Barry asked her.

"Partway," she admitted, "until I couldn't keep up." She grinned sheepishly. "I just wanted to *see* you, Mike, even from a distance. I mean, it's like you're a *celebrity*. I couldn't *help* it. I didn't want to bother you or anything—I guess I'm a nut."

At least she knew it. "Aren't you freezing?" I asked her. My own teeth were still chattering. I put my hand in the open door and touched hers. "Like ice! Come in and get warmed up. We don't want a frozen body on our hands." I helped her out of her car, into the building, and onto the elevator. I was sure Barry was thinking I had *initiation* on my mind. And it did occur to me that Mandy would supposedly do anything for me, but after one touch of her skin, all I could think of was *hot soup.*

I made her a cup of instant noodle while Barry wrapped her up in his one wool blanket. He gave me a glance as if to hint that maybe she was what we'd been looking for. "Forget it!" I hissed under my breath. Hell, Mandy thought I was some kind of hero. How could I ruin her image of me? I made more instant soup and turned on the TV.

To make a long story short, the three of us watched the late movie together. The only touching I did was to massage Mandy's foot when it fell asleep. She was about the last person I could be attracted to, I realized. Punky pink hair doesn't grab me. As an experiment, I pictured Sheila in Mandy's place, but even that didn't turn me on.

When the late movie was over, I walked Mandy down to her Plymouth, and after making sure the motor started, I gave her a quick peck on the cheek. "Look, I'm flattered and all," I said, "but you know I'm going with Sheila. Let's be friends, okay? And after this, please don't drive around like you've been doing. I'll give you one of my yearbook pictures. Won't that be just as good?"

"Now? May I have it now?"

"Sure." Digging one out of my wallet, I signed it, *"To Mandy, with many fond memories of your Plymouth all those nights . . ."*

"Wow, thanks a lot, Mike. I'll stop following you, if you want me to. Thanks for the soup and foot-rub. See you—good night!"

Barry and I talked for a while after that, about Mandy and women in general. The experiences of the night had convinced me I wanted Sheila, not just anyone. How to arrange it, though? I started asking Barry, but he got off on a kick about his townhouses, so after drinking a beer or two to warm me up, I fell asleep with him still talking.

The next morning, Saturday, I woke up with a bad taste in my mouth. The day was very gloomy. Barry had to go to work, so I was in the apartment by myself. About eleven, maybe, the phone rang. "Hello?"

"I. Ronald Schwartz, here, your former business partner."

"Cut it out, man. What's bugging you?"

"You are." He paused. "Only a friend like me would tell it to you straight."

"Tell me what?"

"That you're running around in too many directions. That you're *losing your sense of humor*—"

"I am not."

"Well, then, how about coming over to my house today, to work on our summer plans?"

"Gee, sorry, I can't, I'm meeting this guy for lunch—"

"Some friend of Barry's, right?" Ron guessed. "Watch out, Bronti, watch out. Barry and his buddies are *taking* you, that's what I'm afraid of."

"No, I'm taking *them* to lunch," I snapped. "Besides, it's my business, okay?"

"Okay," Ron said coolly. "Call me whenever you're tired of Barry, which will be soon, I'm predicting. Hey, nother thing. Lennie Thompson's mother died. Martin old me this morning at Freddy's—"

"She did? Of what?"

"I don't know. She was sick. The funeral's today."

I'm still not sure why it hit me so hard, hearing about Lennie's mother, but after I got off the phone with Ronnie, slumped down on Barry's bed. It wasn't as if I knew her or anything. It wasn't as if I even knew Lennie or really iked him. But how did it happen? I wondered. What were heir horoscopes for this week?

I tried to get Lennie and his mom out of my mind, but I kept remembering her odd voice, and those groceries on he sidewalk, and my *dream* that she had died. That was what bothered me the most. Was I clairvoyant, or something? From now on, did I have to worry that all my bad dreams would come true? Maybe that was the penalty I was going to have to pay for being lucky in the lottery. It igured—things evened out. You had to pay for your luck.

I sat around for a few minutes, feeling strange and really onely. There was more than an hour before I was due for unch—a whole hour by myself. Suddenly I didn't think I could stand being alone that long. I needed to be *with* somebody. Was it true that Barry and his friends were using me? No, damn it, it wasn't.

I went into the bathroom and started to shave, but I couldn't shake off my gloominess. In fact, looking at myself n the mirror made me feel worse than before. What was missing? Muttsy. Muttsy had always watched me when I was shaving. I thought about Thompson some more, and then I got an idea.

I got dressed as neatly as possible. This was what you were supposed to do, wasn't it? I went down and got in my car and stopped for a paper at Freddy's News. Back in my car, I looked up the obituary. St. Margaret's Church at noon. Should I go? Yeah, I told myself, I had never really apologized.

I couldn't help thinking as I drove, of last night with Barry in North Glenfield. Just two blocks past the bar with the bouncer was St. Margaret's Church. Two blocks farther ahead would be Farber Street, with its gray sagging porches and people who went shopping before seven so they could get a free carton of milk. I parked the car on the street—behind a few other cars and a hearse—and I went in, crossed myself, and sat down in the back.

Where were the stained-glass windows here, like my church had? There weren't any. Even one of the clear glass panes was broken, which made the place very cold. The service had started. The priest was praying over the closed coffin of Lennie's mother. I could see the back of Lennie's head, where he was sitting in the front row. Did he have a father? I wondered. If his father was there, it wasn't obvious. Who would support him now? He was old enough to be working, but I couldn't imagine Lennie supporting himself. *"The Lord giveth and the Lord taketh away . . . "* Man, some people had no luck.

The priest was speaking in a low voice now, saying something about Lennie's mother. Near my pew in the back there was a box for mass cards. People sometimes gave money, I remembered. If I gave money, would Lennie appreciate it or send it back? No, only my father and sister would do something dumb like that.

Soon the service ended and the small group of people up front started to leave. I quickly scribbled a check to Lennie for two thousand dollars. I wasn't sure what to do with it, but I decided to slip it in with the mass cards. Then I waited to see Lennie as he walked out with the priest. "Lennie? Hi." I put out my hand.

He grabbed it. "Bronti!"

He seemed as surprised to see me now as the day I'd knocked him down. He looked pale and very shaky.

"I'm really sorry," I said. "Was she sick long?"

"Yeah, for about a year. Thanks for coming."

"You're welcome." I paused, remembering that morning. I'd gotten it wrong—he hadn't been afraid of his mom, he'd been just plain afraid. "Look, I'm sorry—I'm sorry for everything. I should have talked to you before I jumped you. I hope you can forget it. I'll be seeing you. Goodbye."

I got in the car and drove—*home*, I was going to say, but Barry's apartment wasn't home, I realized. Not that I was suddenly ready to go back to my parents' house, but I couldn't help *thinking*. What if something bad happened in *my* family, the way it had in Lennie's? It really was dumb to be holding a grudge.

The first thing I did when I got back to Barry's was to cancel my lunch date. I really should be spending more time on my family and old friends, I thought. First I tried calling Amy, but she wasn't in. Next I decided I'd go over in person to see Sheila. And not just because I craved her body. I was going to be more considerate of people from now on.

My grandma, for instance, I was thinking as I drove over to Sheila's. I wasn't even mad at Grandma, so how come I'd cut her off from me too? She was old, much older than Lennie's mom. She could be sick right now and I'd never know it. Meanwhile I parked the car, walked up to Sheila's house, and leaned on the bell. No one came, so after a couple of seconds I rang it again.

Finally the door opened a crack.

I saw a wisp of her hair. "Sheila?"

Her voice was faint when she answered. "I don't want to see you ever again."

"*What?*" I tried to push the door open, but she closed it in my face.

"Hey, come on, Sheila, have a heart!" I called as I banged on the door. "What's wrong? At least *tell* me, *what did I do?*"

20

I stood there, trying to look through the peephole that Sheila's parents had put in the door to check out visitors, but all I could see was a reflection of my eye. Sheila was in there, I was certain, on the other side of the door. I could hear a creaking sound and a sob. "Come on, Sheil," I begged, "please open up?"

She finally did, and I stepped inside before she could change her mind. "I don't get it," I said, baffled. "What are you so upset about?"

She looked at me with red-rimmed eyes. "How *could* you? Didn't you know I'd find out? She *told* me every detail!"

"Who did, about what?"

"Mandy Calise told me everything about you and her last night!"

I was silent for a second. "What did she say?"

"Oh, come on, Mike." Sheila twisted her hair and let out a groan. "Please, I'm sick enough. Don't make me repeat what she said!"

"I want to hear it."

She took a deep breath. "That you're the most amazing, lovable, sensitive, *rich* human being she's ever met—" Sheila's voice broke. "That she spent most of the night last night with you! That you warmed her up and kissed her and fondled her feet!"

"Sheila, wait—when—? Did she call you? How do you know all this?"

"I ran into her at K Mart this morning. She was buying a frame for your picture! *'With many fond memories of your Plymouth . . .'* " Sheila sputtered. "What were you doing in her car?"

"Nothing! Look, it's simple to explain—I wasn't even in it!" It wasn't that simple to explain, though. It took me almost a half hour. Eventually she believed me—that I had only treated Mandy *humanely*, and that the last thing I wanted was to see Mandy's Plymouth. I also told her about going to the funeral, and how it had got me thinking that holding grudges was dumb. "Come on," I begged her, "let's not waste time. Let's enjoy ourselves every minute. Make any kind of a wish and I'll make it come true."

What she wanted most, it turned out, was for us to double date with her cousin Sunny, so after weeks of putting that off, I agreed to her plan right away. The following Saturday we would pick up Sunny and Billy and go around with them while they looked for an apartment. Maybe I'd see one for myself, I thought, one I could rent just for a few months.

During those next couple of days I thought a lot about my parents. I wanted to get in touch with them, but I was too stubborn, I guess you could say. Why didn't they call *me*? If they called, I'd forgive them for everything. So to keep my mind off my troubles, I killed most of my spare time with Barry and his buddies, until Saturday, when Sheila and I went to pick Sunny and Billy up.

"I hope you like each other," Sheila said on the way. "Sunny's not *just* a relative. She's been my best friend since we were little, and—well, I hope Billy will get to be yours."

"Yeah, me, too," I said. I'd been trying like mad to please Sheila ever since the Mandy Calise episode. Mandy was still eyeing me at school in a way that made Sheila suspicious, but at least she was keeping her word about not following me in her car.

"This is Mike!" Sheila introduced me proudly after we pulled up in front of Sunny's house.

"Oh, wow, we've heard so much about you!" Sunny said. "Haven't we, Billy?"

"Yeah."

Sunny looked something like Sheila—not as pretty, but the same type. Blond, with a good figure and a slightly turned-up nose. Billy was into building his body. He lifted weights for three hours every other day, he told me. He was popping out of his suit jacket. "What do you do for a job?" I asked him.

"I have my own gardening service," he said.

"Yeah, Billy's doing really well," Sunny bragged. "Not as well, of course, as *some* lucky people, but we'll be satisfied as long as we can find an apartment we can afford."

So we set out on the search. I was driving, Sheila was next to me, and Sunny and Billy were in the backseat. Even in broad daylight they were sitting so close that you couldn't tell where one ended and the other began. It was nice, seeing two people as much in love as those two.

"Where are we going?" I asked them. "You want to go to a rental agent?"

"No, that costs more money," Sunny said. "I found three apartments without agents advertised in the *Independent.*"

As I drove to the first one, I pulled Sheila close to me.

"When are *you two* going to make an announcement?" Sunny asked us.

"As soon as Sheila wins the lottery," I said. "I want to be sure she isn't marrying me just for my money."

Sheila, laughing a lot, fingered her pearl necklace from Medoff's. "Isn't he terrible, Sunny? Mike, you're too much!"

Billy let go of Sunny for a second to run his hands over my vinyl seat covers. "I wouldn't mind having a Camaro."

"Neither would I!" Sunny said. *"Now* when we go out, we go in Billy's pickup truck."

The first apartment Sunny wanted to look at was in a building at Main and Murchison. "Too noisy," Billy said right away while I was trying to park. "And no garage," he moaned. "Forget it."

"The price is okay, though," Sunny told him. "We may as well look at it, since we're here. 'Ring for superintendent,' " she read from the ad.

An old woman who didn't speak English came to the door.

"See apartment?" Sunny asked her. "Up? Which floor? Where?" The woman shook her head helplessly. "Us see?" We pointed, sounding like Pilgrims trying to talk to the Indians. Finally we gestured our way through the communication barrier, and she led us into an elevator, which took us up to the tenth floor. The apartment was tiny, though.

"Where would I keep my weights?" Billy asked.

And then we discovered another reason not to choose this particular place. It was occupied already by an army of roaches.

"Let's try the next ad, it's for a two-family house," Sunny said as we came down in the elevator. Then, when we were in the car again, the lovebirds started talking about their wedding. "We've still got to narrow our guest list down," Sunny complained.

"Yeah, and because of it, our moms aren't speaking to each other." Billy sighed. "And as of yesterday one of my ushers backed out on me."

"I have a great idea," I said. "Why don't you elope?"

"Oh, no, Mike, we couldn't!"

I could see they were pretty tense because of all these wedding-related problems. That's why I felt really encouraged as we pulled up at the two-family house. "Nice neighborhood, nice place."

"It's so cute, Sunny!" Sheila said.

Billy nodded. "Hey, a basketball hoop on the garage!"

"Look, a baby carriage," Sunny noticed.

"Whoooo! Are you ready for *that*?" I asked them. Sunny and Billy giggled, and Sheila nuzzled against my shoulder. Might be nice, I thought, far away in the future, having my own kid to play basketball with.

We got out and went up the front path. "Look—*grass*," Sunny said, as if she'd never seen any before.

"Yeah, I like grass," Billy agreed. "I mean, being in gardening and all."

Sheila was hanging on to my arm tight. "I love white siding," she whispered. "Look, a private entrance. You'd be living up there, Sunny. How many rooms did it say?"

"Three and a half." Sunny was jumping with excitement as she rang the doorbell.

A man answered. "Yes? Can I help you?"

Sunny coughed. "We—we'd like to see the apartment?"

He took a long look at the four of us. "The newspaper ad says to call first. We're used to making appointments first on the phone."

"Oh, wow, sorry," Sunny apologized. "Since we're here, though, could we—could you—?"

He gave us the once-over again, as if we were aliens from outer space. "This is my house and my wife's. We're looking to rent to a married couple, not a groupie thing."

"Oh, no, you're wrong!" Sunny laughed. "It's only the two of us, and we're *going* to be married!"

"Yeah, they are," I backed her up. "We're just driving them around."

"A quiet business couple," the man added.

"We're very quiet," Sunny told him.

Billy finally spoke. "I got my own business, my own truck and everything."

The man shook his head. "It's rented. Someone already saw it and put down a deposit—"

Sunny let out a little sound. "But—you—you didn't say that before."

"Well, I would have, if you had called first."

"This is age discrimination," I muttered to Billy. "He doesn't want you just because you're young."

"Well, we don't want him, either!" Sunny led us away from the door.

Back in the car we felt bad. It would have been great for them to live there.

"So unfair," Sunny was murmuring.

"The heck with that senile idiot, we'll find something better," Billy said. "Where's the next place? Shall we call this time?"

Sunny checked the ad. "There's no phone number. It's twelve Forman Street, North Glenfield."

"Are you sure you don't want to try an agent?" I asked her. "North Glenfield is kind of depressing."

"I know." Sunny nodded. "Some people can afford to think of those things, but Billy and I can't. We don't have much money. If you're willing to drive us, let's go."

On the way to North Glenfield Sunny and Billy were quiet. Sheila and I tried to be cheery, but in the grayness and traffic of North Glenfield most of our comments fell flat. "Okay, we're on Adams," I told them. "Look for Forman. Is this it?"

"Yeah."

I turned and saw number 12. Oh, no. The apartment advertised in the *Independent* was over the Red Beam Bar. *Forget* it.

It's hard to remember exactly what happened next, as we sat dejectedly in the car in North Glenfield. Sunny was about to cry, Billy was clenching his hands in frustration, and Sheila, trying to buck them up, said, "You'll both probably laugh about all this someday, when you're living in Glenhaven Commons."

"Glenhaven Commons!" Sunny sat up. "We saw an ad for that, remember, Billy?"

"I heard they *want* young people there," Sheila said. "That's the image they're trying to create."

"Glenhaven Commons is apartments, right?" Billy asked.

"No, townhouses," I told him. "I've been hearing about

them in my sleep. My roommate Barry's one of the sales-men."

"They sound fantastic," Sunny said as I started up the motor. "You're right. Maybe someday we'll be able to afford to live there. Meanwhile I guess we'll have to give up and go to an agent. If we can't find an apartment really soon, we'll have to put the wedding off."

"Oh, no," Billy protested, wrapping his massive arms around her.

"You'll find a place," Sheila reassured him.

"Don't be so sure," Sunny said. "Mike, do you know any rental agents?"

"Yeah, but before we go there, let's take a ride. Wouldn't you like to see what the Camaro can do?"

"Yeah, sure," Billy agreed.

So just for kicks, without telling them where I was going, and mostly to shock Barry, I stepped on the gas and headed for Glenhaven Commons. The ride was beautiful. I don't always notice what's going on in nature, but this was the first springlike day, and we passed some nice farms.

"Where *are* we?" they finally asked me when I turned off the farm road.

"I'm just giving you a glimpse of your distant future," I said as we saw the sign GLENHAVEN COMMONS.

The place was doing a great business, judging by all the action in the parking lot. I immediately spotted Barry directing cars around a muddy spot. "I thought you were a salesman!" I called out.

"I'm just working here until the attendant comes back," he said, embarrassed. Then he came over and greeted Sheila and met Sunny and Billy. "So you finally came to your senses, Bronti." He stuck his fist inside the open window and pounded me. "I've been trying to convince this guy for weeks what an opportunity he's missing."

"Now that we've said hello," I told him, "go tend to your serious customers. We just came out to get a breath of fresh air before we head back to see an agent."

"What kind of agent?"

"Apartment rental." I explained about Sunny and Billy tying the knot soon and the trouble we'd been having.

"Man, I sympathize," Barry said. "Age discrimination makes my blood boil. Here we're doing the opposite. We're giving special breaks to young buyers."

"We still couldn't afford it," Sunny said. "I wish, but—"

"Hold on. Here comes the attendant." Barry opened the car door, shoved me over, and motioned for the others to get out while he parked. "I'm not letting you two leave until you see what kind of special deals we're offering."

He proceeded at this point to pull out the red carpet for us. Or to pull out the paper runner, I should say, so that we could cross the muddy parking lot. "Picture thick green lawn where we are now," he said, "sturdy as Astroturf, but real."

"Sounds good to me," Billy said, nodding. "Will they be needing somebody to cut it?"

"I'll find out in the office." Barry took us there next, to see the master plan and the scale models. "When it's finished," he explained, "there'll be one hundred twenty units in all. Plus an Olympic-size pool, tennis courts, garages, health spa—you name it." He waved out the window, at the wooded hills in the background. "Doesn't it remind you of Colorado, less than a half hour from Glenfield?"

"Yeah," Billy agreed enthusiastically.

Sunny smiled. "You've never even *been* to Colorado, Billy!"

Then Barry pointed out his boss, the famous developer Sean Burgess. "I'd love to introduce you to Sean," he said, "but as you can see, he's really tied up today. I'll ask him later about lawn service. Meanwhile you absolutely *have* to see the models." So we trooped outside, past a sign that said POOL WILL BE OPEN TO RESIDENTS MEMORIAL DAY.

"These are finished?" Sunny asked as we approached.

"Yes, these are models."

"I love how each one has a terrace," Sheila said.

"All the terraces face the pool. Yesterday we sold one like that to a twenty-four-year-old banker"—he pointed—"today we sold one of *those* to an actress who's in commercials, and one like *that* to a couple in their twenties, who own this terrific boutique. First, though, before we see the models, you've got to see the spa."

He led us across a plank, over another sea of mud, into the shell of a building that looked like an airplane hangar. "Imagine it finished," Barry said, "racquetball court, indoor track . . ."

"Weight-lifting room?" Billy asked.

"Are you kidding? We're getting a trainer who's a former Mr. Universe. The spa comes free, you know, to anyone who buys in on this special deal." Barry nodded at the other people who were milling around. "That's why we've got such a mob here today. When are you getting married?" he asked Sunny and Billy.

"In less than two months."

"Congratulations!" He shook Billy's hand. "This one unit I'm going to show you is supposed to be done in six weeks. Are you ready to see it?"

174

By this time Sunny and Billy were both panting. So was Sheila. "Sure!"

Barry managed somehow to get us to the head of the line of people waiting. "Only for close friends," he whispered. "The other salesmen will freak out if they find out I put you ahead."

Once we went inside, Sunny and Sheila looked like two characters in a speeded-up movie. "Sheila, come over here!" "Sunny, this bathroom!" "A real fireplace, Mike!" "Look at these *closets*!" they went on, as if closets were a great new invention of Barry's boss. "The bedroom's so big!" "Oh, wow, the kitchen! What's this?"

"A garbage compactor," Barry said, taking credit for each detail as though he had designed the whole place.

What I liked was the skylight. I stood there, looking up at it. Some spot this would be for putting my drawing board. Man, over a month since I'd last seen my own room at home. I needed to start making some time for cartooning. I missed my pens, and my notebooks, and my privacy and—I hated to admit it, but yeah, I was even missing my parents.

Meanwhile, in front of my eyes in the townhouse, a live comic strip was in progress. Barry was telling Billy, "The place comes with a dish."

"Only one?"

"Out there!" Barry pointed to a huge TV dish antenna.

"Oh, wow!" Billy blinked. "Could I get sumo wrestling from Japan?"

It was late by the time we had seen everything in the model. "Well, that's it." Barry rubbed his hands together. "What do you think?"

Sunny shivered. "It's gorgeous!"

"It's my dream house." Billy nodded.

Sheila came over and clutched my arm. "Mike, it's beautiful, isn't it?"

Sunny looked up cautiously at Barry. "How much—is it?"

"Two hundred thousand—"

"Oh." She couldn't pretend to be cool. "I should have known, I guess," she said. "We'd better go. Will any agents still be open?"

"Wait"—Barry stopped her—"that's before the special discount! It's only one-fifty if you buy now and put down twenty thousand cash."

Sunny smiled, but her eyes looked sad. "Billy and I only have a total of three thousand dollars."

"Gee, that's tough," Barry sympathized. "Any chance your parents could help you out? Anybody else you could borrow from? It's worth making whatever arrangements you can. These units can be rented or resold at a profit—"

Rented or resold at a profit . . . Why hadn't I thought of it sooner? I could help them and myself at the same time. "*I'll* buy one," I said.

"Are you *serious*?"

The looks on their faces were priceless. "Sure, I'll rent it to you two, at a price you can afford."

"Mike!" Sunny gasped.

"I love you!" Sheila hugged me.

"Oh, wow, man!" Billy laughed.

"Smart move!" Barry nodded.

That's what money was for, wasn't it? To help out your friends.

21

Whoopee! Aiiiie! "Here's to Mike!" "For he's a jolly good fellow!"

There was nothing I could have done that would have caused a bigger stir at that point. Barry patted my back and went for his boss. Sunny and Billy were all over me, saying, "Mike, you're fantastic! How can we thank you?" And Sheila kissed me passionately in front of everyone, something she doesn't usually do.

Barry came back in a few minutes, his eyes glittering with excitement. "Mike"—he cleared his throat—"I'd like you to meet Mr. Burgess—Sean. This is Mike Bronti," he told his boss. "You may have heard of him—he recently won the New Jersey Pick-Six Lottery."

"Sure, sure, I saw that in the *Independent*—congratulations!" Sean Burgess shook my hand. "Is Louis Bronti your father, by any chance?"

"Yes, he is."

"How about that! Sure, I know Lou. He's been in the business a long time."

"Yeah, he has," I said, surprised, now that I was seeing

Burgess close up. From the way Barry had talked, and from seeing Burgess behind a desk, I was expecting somebody seven feet tall, instead of this guy who was much shorter than I am—with a mustache as scrawny as Ronnie's. Just goes to show a guy can be a success without looking any certain way.

"I'm real glad to meet you," Burgess told me. "Happy you're going to be one of our homeowners. Let's you and I talk for a minute—Barry can entertain your friends. Barry, make sure they're comfortable. Get them coffee or sodas."

I followed Burgess out of the model into his office, where he led me to an easy chair.

"Make yourself comfortable, Mike. Now let me explain how I operate. As soon as I receive your cash deposit, I can finish your unit. Then we'll arrange financing on—"

"Great," I interrupted. "I'm in a big hurry, because I'm going to rent it to my friends, who're getting married in two months. It'll be done by then, won't it?"

Burgess glanced at his calendar. "I'm known for being a fast mover. I've got enough men working this week, so there's no reason I can't go forward. Is your dad going in with you on this?"

"No, he doesn't know about it. I—haven't seen him, actually. I'm living at Barry's." Suddenly I understood something. "I'm—I'm trying to show my dad I can manage my money on my own."

"Good for you. That's the spirit! I can see why you and DeVane hit it off. He's a self-starter. You both are. Now let me ask you this, do you have a lawyer?"

"Yeah, somebody named DeAngelo is my dad's. I'm supposed to be seeing him one of these days."

"I know Tom DeAngelo. Has he advised you about your money?"

"Not yet. I'm advising myself, mainly."

"Good." He sounded impressed. "As soon as I get the twenty-thousand-dollar deposit, we'll sign a contract and I'll finish the unit. How soon can you go to contract—this week?"

"What's wrong with today?"

Burgess sat up. "I thought *I* was a mover! What do you want to do, give me a personal check?"

"Yes." I pulled out my checkbook to show I was serious.

He smiled again. "How do I know you have enough in there to cover it?"

Was he kidding? "All my winnings are still in this account. I'm going to decide where to move them later on this week."

The phone rang at that point, but Burgess ignored it. He leaned forward and folded his hands. "You might want to think about buying more than one unit."

"No, one should be enough, thanks. I'll be leaving for California soon, and I may be putting money down on some land for an amusement park, so I'll write you a check for twenty thousand dollars—"

"Fine." He looked pleased, not used to dealing with customers as decisive as I was. "I'll give you a receipt." He wrote one out, handed it to me, and took my check. "We'll begin immediately to draw up a contract," he said as he shook my hand. "You'll hear from me as soon as your check clears at the bank."

"Great."

"Your friend Barry will work with you directly on the decisions you'll have to make—the color of tiles, carpeting, walls—it's been a pleasure to meet you, Mike. I'm happy we're doing business together." He paused. "You're sure you won't be seeing your father?"

I had just decided about that. "When this is all settled."

Burgess paused. "Well, when you do, be sure to tell him hello from me."

"I will. So long, Mr. Burgess." We shook hands again and I left.

Barry insisted, after that, on taking all four of us out to dinner, so that Sunny said, "Whoever hangs around with Mike Bronti sure gets treated right!" During dinner I assured her and Billy that I would charge them rent that they could afford, and then, after Barry had paid the bill, Sheila and I drove Sunny and Billy home.

"There's no way to thank you, Mike!" Sunny gushed when we dropped them off at her place.

"Wait a second," Billy said, "I just thought of a way. Mike, would you be in our wedding? We need an usher, and there's nobody we feel closer to now than you."

How could I say no to that? "Sure," I agreed. "Talk to you soon—good night." Then Sheila and I went on, finally alone.

I don't know if it was because of spending the day with the lovebirds or just general pent-up emotions, but at that moment I craved Sheila's body so badly I could hardly concentrate on driving the car. When we got to her house, I turned off the motor and pounced on her, literally, and for the first time in her life Sheila seemed as eager as I was.

We got as close as we'd ever been, let's say, without going into a whole story. Picture us, giving off electrical sparks—*fffssst, bzzz, zap, wow!* The car was cramped and all that, but that didn't even bother me. I was on the brink of one of life's most important moments . . . so I thought. And then suddenly Sheila pulled away. "Mike," she said breathlessly, "we've got to talk."

"Talk?" I moaned, every part of my body nearly exploding. *"Please*, Sheila," I begged, and tried to grab her again.

"No, wait!" She drew back farther. "I want to as much as you do, Mike! But let me say this—I've got an idea, since this afternoon . . ."

Sinking down in the seat, I crossed my legs painfully. "Go on, go on, *talk*."

She reached for my hand and played with my fingers. "Sunny and Billy are so lucky."

That's what she had to tell me? "Yeah, well, I like helping people."

Sheila moved a little closer. "They're going to be together all the time. I envy them, you know?"

"You can come to California."

"I've got a better idea," she said. "You could buy another Glenhaven townhouse, and we could be neighbors of Sunny and Billy."

"That'd be a rough daily commute, from Glenhaven Commons to Los Angeles."

Sheila took a deep breath. "I mean, you could go to Glenfield Community instead, like I'm going to do. You could study business. Isn't that what your dad wants? Maybe you'd get along better with him if you did that. And we'd be together all the time."

Hmm. I looked at her in the dim light. "Wouldn't your parents—be upset?"

"About what?"

"I mean, us living together . . ."

"We'd be married! How could they object to that?"

"Oh." I swallowed. *Gleep.*

"Mike, we love each other," she went on, massaging my chest with the tips of her fingers. "Most young couples who love each other have to wait because they're broke. I want to live together, to *be* together in the way you're thinking, but only if we're married. How about it? We could do it after school's over, at the beginning of the summer."

She touched my lips with her fingertips and then kissed me very gently. "I'll—I'll think about it," I stammered. "It would solve certain problems.... Let's keep it to ourselves, though, while I think about it. What do you say?"

"Okay."

I hadn't been planning on a move like that, but as we went into another clinch, my leaping hormones sent me the message that the idea wasn't bad.

I was pretty mixed up after I left her and went on to Barry's. What did I want, Cummings and travel or the comforts of home? And where was home, the lot at Glenhaven, or my fold-out bed at Barry's, or my room at my parents' house? I was going to have to make some major decisions, I thought as I stopped at a traffic light.

When I got to Barry's place, he was waiting for me, still high on salesmanship. I envied him for being able to get such a kick out of that. I remembered my dad selling a big office building once and acting as if he'd hit a World Series grand slam. Maybe *I* could learn how to get that kind of thrill out of business, if I took up accounting at Glenfield Community.

Anyway, Barry went on, talking about ways to make money. I would rather have talked about women, but he was caught up in BUCKS. "Don't charge Sunny and what's-his-name too little rent," he said. "You have to cover your mortgage and maintenance."

"Yeah, yeah, good night," I said, worn out. "Talk to you about it tomorrow."

We couldn't sleep very late that next morning, because Barry was working again, even though it was Sunday. Just before he left, the phone rang and he said, "Bronti, for you."

"Hello?"

"Mike—thank God I got you."

"Grandma?" *Grandma!*

"How you *doing*?"

"I'm fine, what about you? I was thinking of calling you—"

"Sure, sure—quit thinking about it and get over here," she said. "I went to church early and I'm home. I made lasagne. Hurry up. Just you and me. Are you coming?"

"Yeah, okay, okay, Grandma, I'll be over right away."

I felt relieved as I got dressed. My guilt trip was heavier than I'd been admitting. Plus it was nice to know that someone in the family had finally called me up. Maybe this was a trick, I considered. She'd have my parents there too. So what, I didn't care. In a way I almost hoped she would.

"Hi." I felt really strange when I first saw my grandma. It was only a month or so since I'd seen her, but she seemed shorter somehow.

"I should give you a couple of good ones," she said, chopping the air with her hand. "But you're too big to hit and I'm getting too old. Sit, you fresh kid." Grabbing me by the ears, she pulled me down on the couch and kissed me, leaving a red print, as usual. "Is this money making you crazy or something? If it is, throw it away!"

"I'm not crazy," I said. "It's not the fault of the money. Dad was coming down too hard on me and I figured I'd give him a break. If I'm not home, it's easier on him." I paused. "How are they doing?"

She jiggled my hands in hers impatiently. "Dumb bunny, you're asking me? Go see for yourself!"

"How did you find out where I was?" I asked.

"Well, I knew your daddy and mom knew, but they wouldn't tell me nothing. You'll come to your senses pretty soon, they said—you're basically a good kid. But I couldn't wait no more. So I *investigated*. I remembered your friend's name, Linganelli, and I bought five pounds of veal . . ."

"You offered Lingo a bribe to tell you where I was?"

"What are you talking about? No bribes. You'll bring your friend over some night this week for a nice Italian meal, that's all."

"So how are Mom and Dad doing?" I asked again when we were at the table eating lasagne.

Grandma refilled my dish. "To me, he's like a—a person dragging himself. He hasn't sold those, those elephants they stuck him with. He ought to get out of that office."

"I wanted to help—"

"Yeah, yeah, and you wanted to give him a car, and he said no." Her eyelids drooped, like the eyelids of Garfield the cat. "That's how he is, stubborn, like you are. Ask him again about a business, why don't you? Something for you and him to be in together."

"You think he'd listen now?"

"I don't know. He's *missing* you, I'm telling you. Go home and tell him you miss him. What kind of a nut are you acting like, eh? You haven't even talked to your sister! You know what she's doing this week? What do you call it—she's *fasting*! Can you tell me how her starving herself *here* is going to help kids in Africa? Come on," she said in the same breath, "have some more sauce meat. You're two good, smart kids—why don't you stop all this crazy stuff? Life's short, Mike, believe me. Go make up with Mom and Daddy."

"I will."

It wasn't only what Grandma said—I'd been thinking of seeing them. Now that I'd heard my dad was missing me, I thought of a plan. I left Grandma, promising to patch things up with them soon. But first I had some arranging to do. So, my dad might accept an offer to go into business with me now? All riiight! Bronti and Father, Incorporated. I got back into my car.

To make a long story short, I went back to Glenhaven Commons. First I found Barry, who took me to Burgess again, and I gave Burgess another check. Sixty thousand dollars was a lot to put down, but I would own not one but *three* brand-new townhouses. Even if it turned out that Sheila and I lived in Glenhaven, someone would have to manage the other two or else take care of reselling them. That was the deal I'd offer my dad—being my partner in real estate.

22

After I'd written a second check for forty-thousand dollars to Burgess, he gave me another receipt. "As soon as both your checks clear," he told me again, "we'll get together, you, me, and our lawyers. Listen, I happen to be seeing Tom DeAngelo tomorrow. I'll save you the trouble and arrange the meeting with him. Are you still keeping all this a surprise for your dad?"

"Yeah. I'll tell him about it when it's all done. How long will it take for the checks to clear?"

"Oh, just a day or two, I think. It's a local bank and they always give me good service."

Barry was treating me like a hero now that I'd bought the three units. "You've made my career, man," he said, "and I'm not only talking about the commission I'll be getting. Since I brought you in, Sean has a lot more confidence in me. He's talking about giving me my own office. Thanks"—he crunched my hand—"I'll remember this when *I'm* rich."

Meanwhile, standing in Sean's office, looking out of the window, I could survey the three spots where my town-houses would be built. Even though one was only partly done and the other two were just on the drawing board, I felt like Yertle the Turtle. Yertle's this character in a Dr. Seuss story, who crawls up on the backs of a huge pile of other turtles, until he's at the top—the king of the pond. That's where I was.

That evening, Barry sat around his apartment with a calculator, figuring out what my monthly payments would be.

"Three thousand . . . let's see, you might have to borrow on your next year's lottery check. . . . There's no risk, though. You'll be getting a rental income. And you could always sell one, or two, or all three."

I didn't mention the possibility of Sheila and me living in one of them. What would my parents think? I wondered. The next day I appeared in school, but I couldn't concentrate on anything. My mind was on Sheila versus Cummings, on blue carpets versus tan carpets, and on making the announcement to my parents that I was a real estate mogul.

That night when Barry came home, he said, "Your checks cleared already. I heard Sean talking to your bank. He said he'll see you tomorrow. He's working it out with DeAngelo. Congratulations, man!"

"Great, I'll call him from school to find out when."

By now I was impatient. I'd stalled long enough with my parents. *Go see them tonight,* I told myself, and right then and there I made some excuse to Barry and went out and got in my car. On the way home I felt nervous, a good kind of nervousness, though. And when I rang the bell and waited, whistling to cover my nervousness, I could hear Muttsy charging the door and barking and jumping up.

My mom opened. Her hands were wet, and so were her

eyelashes, once she saw it was me. Dropping the dishtowel she was holding, she gave me a big hug.

"Hi." We stood there swaying together for a minute. Then I knelt down and petted Muttsy.

My mom smiled and wiped her eyes. "I wasn't sure how you felt about *us*, but I knew you'd come back to see Muttsy."

"Who is it?" my dad called.

My mom led me quietly into the living room, where my dad was sitting at his desk. I grabbed his hand awkwardly before he looked up. "It's me," I said. "Hi, Dad."

He smiled lopsidedly. "Well, the return of the native."

I shifted my weight. "I thought I'd come back—and see how things were going."

"About time!" He got up.

The three of us smiled a little awkwardly and then got into a huddle, like we had on the day when I'd won the lottery.

My dad slapped my back. "Let's hit the kitchen," he suggested. "I could use a cup of coffee."

"You look thin. Have you eaten?" my mom asked me.

"Not really."

"Let me get you something," she offered. "One person fasting in this family is enough."

"How's Amy?"

"Well, we're worried about her, frankly. Of course, we were worried about you, too. Nothing new, right? Profound worry seems to be a permanent condition of parenthood. How have you been?"

"I'm fine, no kidding. It's been a long time away, though. How come you didn't call me?"

My dad rubbed his chin. "We thought a little vacation might do us all good."

"He's kidding!" my mom said. "He missed you more than I did. You think he's this mean, tough character, right? Forget it, he's been miserable." She paused. "We didn't call you, even though we wanted to, because we thought it had to be your decision to come back."

"I figured he'd come back when he spent all his money," my dad grunted. "Well, *did* you?"

"Not all of it ... I decided on an investment, though."

"*Finally!*" My dad poured coffee. "You worked it out with Phil? What did you decide?"

"I didn't go to Phil. I—I decided, by myself, to invest in real estate."

"*Oh?*" My dad and mom exchanged a glance.

"What are you thinking of buying?" my dad asked. "I've still got two *unusual* commercial buildings I can get for you cheap."

"I put deposits on three townhouses at Glenhaven Commons," I said.

"Three?" they both repeated.

"Yeah, I got a special deal from Sean Burgess. Says he knows you. You know him, don't you?"

"I've met him." My dad put down his cup. "You already went ahead with this? What did you give him, a binder? A few hundred dollars?"

"No, I wanted to get things going. I gave him sixty thousand."

He stared like some big bird. "Sixty *thousand*? You had Tom DeAngelo with you, didn't you?"

"Not yet, but don't worry. We're meeting tomorrow. Mr. Burgess arranged it with DeAngelo, and—"

My dad looked at me quizzically. "Let me get this straight. You already gave money to Burgess?"

"Yeah, two checks. Don't worry, I have receipts."

"But no contracts? Tom DeAngelo went along with this?"

"Yes, I said don't worry! I bought three so I can rent them, or resell at a big profit." I figured I wouldn't say anything at the moment about Sheila and me. "What I'm hoping," I began, a little nervous now that I was actually asking him, "is—would you—you know, *help* me with these things, go into business with me?"

"Go into business with you? Help you in real estate?" He cleared his throat. "Okay."

I was shocked. I had expected at least a thousand *ifs*, *ands*, and *buts*. I stuck out my hand, not like before, but like a businessman clinching a deal. My dad smiled as he shook hands, and my mom got all emotional. "I knew you'd patch things up!" she said. "You're both stubborn, but in the end you always come through!"

Of course, we kept talking after that, and the *ifs*, *ands*, and *buts* came up.

"I can't figure why in the hell you gave him so much money before a contract," my dad said. "The receipts are something, but that's not the way it's done."

My mom was afraid we'd start arguing again. "There must be some explanation."

"I'll give DeAngelo a call later," my dad said. "Well, some people think Burgess is a genius—he sure does things his own way. Let's put it this way—I'm agreeing to give you a hand to keep you from making rash moves like this!"

Then he asked a million questions about how the townhouses were built and about interest rates. "I'm not trying to bug you," he told me, "I just want to see if you know what you're doing. The idea of putting your money in real estate makes sense, but you've got to know what you're talking about. Of course, it's *your* money. I still say that. The major decisions are going to be *yours*, buddy. I'm keeping my regular job. Think of me as a part-time consultant."

After a while my dad went back to his desk, but my mom and I kept talking. She was interested in what the townhouses looked like and exactly where they were and all that. I ended up telling her about Sunny and Billy and me being in their wedding. "You don't have any ideas like that in mind for yourself, do you?" she asked me.

I didn't feel like getting into that, so I said, "No, no, not too soon."

"There's a ton of mail for you upstairs," she told me. "It's all in three cartons. You probably won't recognize your room—I had the cleaning service do a job."

"I'll take a look," I said, and Muttsy and I went upstairs. Seeing my room made me feel strange—first of all, the shock of how neat it was, as if I'd died and they'd gotten rid of things that might remind them of me, like dirty socks, and cupcake wrappers, and overdue books from the library. The important stuff was still there, though, and if I'd been like my mother, I would have been bawling my head off because I was that happy to see my drawing board. Okay, effective immediately, I was moving back in.

I sat on my bed for a while, after that, opening envelopes. Over the past weeks a lot more letters had come for the fund. *Dear Mike, How about buying me a Jaguar?* ... *Dearest Michael, I'm available* ... And then I saw one with a return address I recognized: 140 Farber. *Mike*, it said, *Thanks for the check you left in church for me. I had this feeling I should spend it on lottery tickets, but my aunt said no way. The money will help a lot till I find a job. It's hard with my mom gone. Thanks again, and sorry I bugged you. See you around, Lennie.*

Then I saw another envelope with Amy's handwriting on it. When I opened it, there were both of the checks I had sent her, with a note. *Dear Mike, We need this badly. From a stranger I'd accept it. But from you I hate the idea that you're just absolving your guilt. If you really want us to have it, come down and meet the group, and at least see who you're contributing to. I still have hopes for you. Your patient sister, Amy.*

"What's that?" my mom called upstairs.

"Nothing," I told her. Actually, it was me, moaning pitifully. Was Amy right, that lucky people like me should share, share, share, share? Would it really improve the world? Or was improving the world hopeless, even for a millionaire? Maybe I shouldn't have bought the townhouses, which would only help a few people live better.

For the rest of the evening I sat around listening to old phone messages and calling people. Until now I'd kept quiet about my three-townhouse deal. When I told Sheila, she went wild. "My dad'll be thrilled that you spent in Glenfield, but I'm even happier—oh, Mike, this means you're not going to California!"

Wasn't I? I still hadn't decided, but for the time being I would let her be happy thinking I wasn't going. When I called Barry, he said he'd miss me as a roommate and he congratulated me again for my super-sharp business sense. Only Ron complained that my townhouses were a stupid purchase. "I'll make a profit on them," I insisted. "They'll help us finance the park!"

When my parents came up to bed, they stopped at my bedroom. "I'm really glad to have you back," my mom told me. "Let's not let anything like that happen again."

"Oh, I don't know," my dad said. "You have to admit it was pretty peaceful around here."

"Come on." I slapped his palm, like a friend this time instead of a business partner. "A little respect from now on. Remember, I'm your boss."

23

      It felt great, being home. Before I went to sleep, I sat at my drawing board. What I drew was a hodgepodge of townhouse layouts and ideas for Brontisaurus Park. Things would be okay now between me and my parents, I figured. They hadn't even mentioned any rules. It was obvious that they were beginning to see me as a responsible adult.

That next morning at breakfast we were all in a good mood. My mom made me an omelet. My dad showed me an article about the outlook in residential real estate. He didn't say one negative thing to me. He only said calmly, "I couldn't reach DeAngelo. You're seeing him today?"

"Yeah."

"You're not missing school, are you?"

"I'll try not to. I'm calling Burgess from school this morning to find out when we're meeting. Want to come?"

"Sure. I'll be in the office all day. Give me a call when you know what time it's set for."

"I'll do that." I got up from the table and put on my jacket. "Speak to you later, so long!"

The first time I tried calling from the school pay phone, Burgess's office wasn't even open yet. I let the phone go for about twenty rings and then I went on to class.

"I forgot to ask you last night," Ronnie said when we met in the hall, "did you get your orientation schedule for Cummings?"

"Maybe, I don't know. I didn't have time to read all my mail."

Ron looked at me angrily. "You're not going to Cummings, are you?"

I hesitated. "What do you mean, I'm not going?"

"I heard all about it from Sheila."

"Heard *what*?"

"About *you* being a June groom. Ain't that sweet, building a nest . . . *giving up your whole future!* How can you do it?" Ron fumed. "After all our years of talking about the park and weeks of planning the trip!"

I gulped. "Wait a minute . . . when? When did you hear this? Sheila told you we were getting *married*?"

"Not me personally. I overheard her telling people right here in the hall. Most of them were really happy for her. Only Mandy Calise was in tears."

"It's not for sure," I said. "We were just sort of playing around with the idea." Damn, so *embarrassing*. How could Sheila blab when I'd asked her not to? How could she do that to me?

I tried to find her after class to tell her a thing or two, but by the time I caught up with her, she was in home ec and the door was shut. Damn, I was annoyed! Instead of going to my next class, I stopped to call Burgess's office again. "Mr. Burgess is out just now," a secretary said. "May I please take a message?"

"Is Barry DeVane in?" I asked.

"Just a moment, please. Mr. DeVane is also out at the moment. Who should I say called?"

I let out my breath—*ffftt!* "Michael Bronti, their biggest client!"

During gym class three people congratulated me because they'd heard I was getting married. "Sheila was kidding," I told them. Man, she'd die if she heard me say that. I couldn't have been more confused. On the one hand, I *loved* her and I didn't want to hurt her. But I also wanted to travel, and go to Cummings Institute, and mainly, I wanted time to make up my own mind!

After gym I tried Burgess for the third time, but again nobody answered. Had Burgess already told me where and when we'd meet and I'd forgotten what he said? At Tom DeAngelo's, maybe? I went to one more class, but after that I was feeling too jumpy, so I left school before lunch and drove over to DeAngelo's office.

Wow, fancy layout. Thick carpet. Lots of framed diplomas. Luckily, nobody around but a secretary. "I'm Mike Bronti. Is Mr. DeAngelo in?" I asked at the front desk. In my sweater and jeans, I felt like Archie Andrews coming to see Daddy Warbucks.

"One moment, please." She gave him a buzz and then told me I could go in.

"Hello, Mike, good to meet you!"

DeAngelo was younger than I had expected, with curly brown hair and glasses.

He got up and shook me hand. "Congratulations on your win. I heard all about it from your dad."

"Nice to meet you," I said. "I'm sorry it took me so long to get around to coming here. Uh, I'm supposed to be in school right now, but I wanted to make sure—did Sean Burgess set up a time for today with you?"

DeAngelo looked puzzled. "Sean Burgess? The builder? Start from the beginning, I think I missed something."

"Didn't Burgess talk to you about signing a contract or something? He told me he'd set it up with you for today."

"Burgess told you what?"

"That he was setting up—"

DeAngelo shook his head. "I'll have Joan check the appointment book, but—"

"It's got to be, he *told* me. He didn't say a time, but— you *know* Burgess, right?"

"No, I don't. I know he's building that development out there called Glenhaven Commons."

"He told me he knew you." I cleared my throat. "I gave him checks that already cleared—deposits on town-houses—totaling sixty thousand dollars."

DeAngelo's mouth was a huge O. He pulled out a chair for me. "Sit down."

His tone made my heart thump. I heard him ask his secretary to try various numbers. Then I sat helplessly while he asked different people questions on the phone. All the while, the expression on his face made my heart do a drum roll. Finally he put in a call to the *Glenfield Independent.*

"Rob?" he said. "Tom DeAngelo. What's this I'm hearing about Sean Burgess? Yeah? When? It's in tonight's paper? Unbelievable. Yeah, yeah." He went on a little longer like that, and then he hung up and swiveled around to face me. "Sorry, Mike, it looks like Burgess skipped town last night with a half million in his clients' money."

When I finally got out of DeAngelo's office, I stopped for a newspaper. Not at Freddy's. I couldn't bear the thought of seeing anyone I knew. I yanked the newspaper off a newsstand and stumbled back to my car. Then I sat inside, reading what the article said.

> Local homebuyers, business associates, and the wife of Sean R. Burgess, Glenfield real estate developer, all reacted with shock today to the news of Burgess's sudden disappearance. Partial evidence available at press time suggests that Burgess may have fled Glenfield with upwards of one-half million dollars in deposits and escrow funds paid by buyers for luxury townhouses, most of which have yet to be started at Burgess's Glenhaven Commons development.
>
> According to Burgess's wife, Virginia R., her husband was expected at home at 10 P.M. last night, and when he failed to arrive by morning, she contacted the Glenfield police. Since 10 A.M. today, when Glenfield officer Larry Felson identified a car at Newark International Airport as Burgess's Lincoln Continental, the assumption is being made that Burgess has fled the country.

It was a long story for the *Independent* and full of guesses about things they hadn't proven yet. It said there was no indication of Burgess having a previous criminal record, but that certain local businessmen had long questioned some of his practices. The authorities were pretty certain he hadn't met with foul play. His wife was shocked more than anyone, because, in addition to clients' money, he had withdrawn all the money in their joint bank accounts. The district attorney was guessing that Burgess had had business and gambling losses and had left before his creditors could close in on him.

Flown the coop with my sixty grand, the bastard! "I'm a fast mover," he had told me. So that's what he'd meant! I beat my head against the steering wheel. Maybe they'd catch him, I thought. "Let me call your dad for you," Tom had offered. "No," I'd insisted, forcing myself to act calm. "I'll go over to my dad's office and tell him myself." What was this going to mean? I asked myself. First of all, it meant that most of my ninety-four thousand was gone, and I still hadn't given anything to the people who had written to the fund. But losing the money wasn't the worst of it—I felt like such a jerk!

There was lots more to the article. I read on a little farther. It told how a friend of Burgess's, a lawyer, had been holding buyers' money supposedly in safekeeping, which Burgess then took. Plus this past weekend he had taken cash directly from an uninformed young buyer—me! It said that further building couldn't go on, since Burgess had been on the verge of bankruptcy, and that the district attorney was going to try to get him, but if Burgess had already left the country, there wasn't much hope—the money would be lost.

I was blind with anger as I sat there reading the rest of it. I felt incredibly stupid, even though other people had been bitten too: "Burgess's generally favorable reputation, plus the special prices he was offering, made Glenhaven Commons seem attractive." Not to mention, on top of that, that Burgess had known my dad. And how could Barry have let me get into this? Barry! Where was Barry? He had led me by the nose and made me lose my money, and now he was probably lolling on a Caribbean beach with Burgess, enjoying my bucks!

Move! I ordered myself. May as well face my dad and

get the explaining over with. DeAngelo had told me I ought to report what had happened to me to the D.A. Wait a minute, though. . . . What if Barry hadn't run off but was still hanging around here? If I couldn't get my hands on the King of the Crooks, I could at least try for the Prince. It was a long shot, I realized. The newspaper article had said that Burgess Company employees were being questioned at their homes. I drove as fast as I could to Barry's apartment. Good, his car was there in the lot. That had to mean he was in.

Instead of waiting for the elevator, I ran up three flights and rang. *Come on, man, what's keeping you?* I knocked. No light under the door, no sounds. My first hunch must be right—he had gone to the airport with Burgess! I knocked and rang again, and at that point I remembered I was still carrying a key to the place.

Digging it out, I opened the door. It was dark in his one-room apartment. The only thing visible was a shimmering TV screen, with just the picture on, no sound. "Hey!" I said. "Barry!" He wasn't here, obviously, but to see the evidence better, I turned on the main ceiling light.

"Mike," he said dully from where he sat slumped in his foam chair.

I jumped. "*Iiiaah!* You're *here!* Thanks for letting me in, buddy. And thanks even more for hooking me up with Burgess, *genius* businessman!"

"You heard," he croaked.

I went over and grabbed his collar. "I sure as hell did! What's *your* story? Why'd you let me? You must've known what he was into, why'd you let me lose my shirt?"

He hid his face. "I knew *nothing!* He conned all of us, even his wife! I'm sorry, man," Barry murmured. "If I had it, I'd pay you back out of my own money. As it is"—he shook his head—"I'm much worse off than you."

He looked awful, I saw as I stared at him. I had come here wanting vengeance, but seeing Barry depressed, slumped in his chair, was throwing me off. "What were you doing here in the dark?"

"*Thinking.*"

"Watching TV with no sound?"

"It's Channel Thirty," he muttered, "the only station that's covering news about Sean. How come the networks aren't carrying it?"

"Because Sean's just a small-time punk!"

Barry winced.

"You had no clue about what he was up to?"

He shook his head mournfully. "Looking back on it, you could say . . . he owed me two weeks' salary. He said he had a cash-flow problem and would pay me this week. Plus my commission from the sales to you—I still had that coming." He rubbed his forehead. "I knew it was unusual for him to take so much money from you up front, but you *offered* it to him." He slumped deeper. "I'm out of a job."

"Yeah, that's rough."

Barry sat up. "I admired the guy! Hell, he was like a—"

"A father to you?"

He sniffed. "Yeah! He said he was giving me my own office. I can't believe he isn't coming back."

After being so furious, I suddenly felt bad for Barry. Having his hero crumble in front of him was like losing one of his parents. Worse, probably, for him, because his parents weren't even involved in his life. I sat down on the edge of the bed now. "What's the latest on Channel Thirty?"

Barry spoke in a monotone. "They're saying he left the

country. It's got to be true. He had just gotten a new passport—said he might be taking his wife on a foreign cruise."

"Have they questioned you?" I asked him.

"Yeah. I told them what I could, which was practically nothing. Sean's last words to me, by the way, were to thank me again for bringing you in." Barry groaned, "I feel like hell. I worked so hard for that guy! Man, do I have a headache. Turn off the light and the TV. I don't want to see any more!"

It was insane. I had come for revenge, and now what was I doing? Getting aspirin for Barry and trying to cheer him up. Before I left, I wrote him a check for five hundred dollars. "Here, take it easy. Use this until you get a new job." Then I left him with the light on, staring at a blank TV screen. Get going, I told myself. Too depressing, staying here. But going to my dad's office would be depressing too. I couldn't. I couldn't face him this minute. I decided to go home.

Great, no one was there except Muttsy, who was as happy to see me as usual. So nice—no matter how dumb you've been, your dog never knows. What I needed now was privacy, a chance to think before my parents came home. With Muttsy behind me, I went up to my room and sat down on my bed. I could imagine my dad, when he learned about Burgess: *I can't believe you didn't know better. Since you were a kid you've heard me talking about contracts! I thought from the start there was something fishy here. How could you be so dumb!*

Now, Louis, my mom would defend me, *it's only money. He's learned a lesson.*

At the rate this kid learns lessons, he may have some smarts by the time he's ninety years old!

I couldn't take hearing what I knew they'd say. And they'd be *right*, that was the worst of it. I *had* been an idiot. Not only with investments, but with practically every aspect of my life. Sheila, for instance. There was no way to do right by her. I wasn't ready to get married, but if I left her, she'd be miserable. Amy! I'd hurt Amy so that she didn't even want my money, and I'd hurt Lennie Thompson physically, by being a macho jerk. Sunny and Billy, the list was endless. Because of my losing my money they were out an apartment. They'd probably have to postpone their wedding or else live over the Red Beam Bar. I had avoided Loyal Lingo and admired Barry the Braggart. And Ronnie—good old Ronnie—I'd kept giving him false hopes about the amusement park. Lynne—I hadn't spoken to her in a couple of weeks, and what about the people who had written me letters? I had left myself with practically nothing to send out from the Bronti Fund.

I should deal with the mail, I really should, I thought, even if I just answered everybody: *Thanks for your interest in the Bronti Fund. Unfortunately, due to his unbelievable stupidity, Mr. Bronti won't be able to make any money gifts until next year.* Right now I should make a list of them and start making up a letter. With that in mind, I got up and dragged the three cartons of mail to the side of my bed.

Man, what a collection. I sat down again and pored over envelopes. Most of them had New Jersey postmarks, but some were from other states. Hey, California—from Cummings! It must be my orientation material. I opened it.

Dear Mr. Bronti,
    Since the acceptance deadline has now passed and we have received no response from you regarding your admis-

sion to Cummings Institute, we assume that you have made other plans for next year. Owing to the number of applicants on our waiting list, we cannot hold places open any longer. If we can be of service to you in the future, please be in touch with us. In the meantime our best wishes for your success in the path you have chosen to follow.

Yours truly,
Patricia P. Sloan
Director of Admissions

What? What were they talking about, no response? I'd sent their card in with a check! What kind of idiots couldn't keep their records straight? I remembered filling it out. My canceled check, that would show them! I charged to my desk and opened the drawers. Where were the canceled checks—still unopened in one of the cartons, probably. So much mail had come while I was at Barry's. I began searching through the boxes for an envelope from Glenfield State Bank. Before I found it, though—damn!— something else turned up first: my acceptance check to Cummings. It had gotten mixed up with the incoming mail and *had never gone out.*

I collapsed on my bed and reread the latest letter: ... *we cannot hold places open any longer.* The words, this time around, hit like a punch in the gut. The longer I looked at them, the more I knew what I wanted. Forget townhouses and investments and going in with my father. What I'd wanted my whole life was to be in commercial art! I would beg Cummings to take me, I'd call and explain the circumstances. The Cummings offices would still be open. It was three hours earlier there. I grabbed the phone and dialed.

"Good afternoon, Admissions, Cummings Institute ..."

"Hello, I'm Mike Bronti," I said hoarsely. I'll skip the details of our conversation. They were sorry, they said. All they could do was to put me last on the waiting list of two hundred twenty people. How many might eventually get in? I asked. Well, last year it had been twelve. Would I like to be number two-twenty-one? No, *thanks*. I hung up.

So. No Cummings in September. And because of Burgess, no townhouse with Sheila, to sweeten up Glenfield Community. No Bronti and Father Realtors, to get my dad out of his slump. I hadn't heard from Murray State yet, but even if I got in, what was the use of it? Losing the money wasn't so bad—in the long run I would still be rich. But what about next year? I wanted to study cartooning, at Cummings, not just anywhere. And I wanted my parents to respect me, not see me as a gullible fool.

I couldn't face them this evening, let alone for the days, weeks, and months ahead of us. Well, who said I had to? I still had some money. I could always go away. I could go off right now, before they came home. Where to? What did it matter? I got up and started throwing things into a bag.

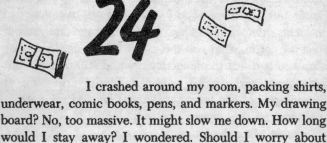

24

I crashed around my room, packing shirts, underwear, comic books, pens, and markers. My drawing board? No, too massive. It might slow me down. How long would I stay away? I wondered. Should I worry about graduating? No. I had been going to school all these years and look how dumb I still was. Okay, *where* to go? That was the question. A couple of pictures formed in my head. One involved Sheila and the other involved Ron.

Okay, my checkbook. I needed my checkbook, without which none of this would be possible. How much was left of my ninety-four thousand? About ten thousand bucks. Not bad. So, *go, before your parents come.* I was still bouncing around frantically. *Take the mail along,* I decided. I'd answer some letters from the road. I loaded the cartons in the car and went back to my room. Anything else? Yeah. I pulled out most of the eighteen gifts from the bank that were still in my closet and loaded them, too.

My final move may seem crazy, I'm the first one to admit it. All the time I'd been getting ready, Muttsy had been following me. My mom had told me that Muttsy had been miserable the whole month I was at Barry's. Why put Mutts through that again? I'd take her along.

I put her in the car and left a note in my room for my parents.

Dear Mom and Dad,
  By the time you see this, I'm sure you'll know about Burgess. I was dumb about him and other things, but I won't feel better by sticking around to hear that from everyone. I realize losing money isn't that terrible, Mom, and I've learned a lesson already, *from Burgess*—that if things are bad here and you can afford it, you may as well leave town. Don't worry, I won't do anything dangerous and I'll let you know where I am, eventually. You may not believe this, but I care about you both—Grandma and Amy, too.
                              Love,
                              Mike

By this time I had a couple of alternative plans in mind. I left the house and went out and joined Muttsy. "Okay, girl, here we go." My first stop was at Sunny's place. Since I'd let Billy and her down with the townhouse, and I wouldn't be around to be in their wedding, I thought the least I could do was to leave them my gifts from the bank. No one was home, which was just as well. I unloaded the cartons and left them on Sunny's porch.

The car felt light after I left Sunny's. I was beginning to feel light myself. I needed a break like this from school and from trying to please everyone. It would be enough, for a while, to get away from all the forces pulling on me and to try to please just *one* other person. Why be annoyed with Sheila? All she'd done was to love me. I would forgive her for having such a big mouth, I decided as I drove to her house.

I parked the Camaro and walked to her door. Sheila should be home from school by now. It was late afternoon. *Let her be home alone,* I prayed silently as I leaned on the bell. I just couldn't face her parents' questions about the Sean Burgess disaster and how it would affect me. They were sure to have heard about it. Everyone had. Besides, I needed privacy like I'd never needed it before, to ask Sheila something big.

The door opened and Sheila fell into my arms. "Mike, I've been trying to call you. I'm so upset! So are my parents. We've been watching Channel Thirty news. How could Burgess *do* that to you? Why did you go along with him? My dad says there are lots better townhouses you could have bought!"

"Hey, don't make me feel worse than I do." I ran my hands through her hair. "Look, can we talk alone?" Too late. Her parents had heard my voice and were already rushing into the hall.

"Poor Mike!" Mrs. Cooke sighed.

"You said it!" Mr. Cooke shook his head. "Rich Burgess and poor Mike. You wrote him a check, Mike, for how much? You handed it over just like that?"

"Maybe they'll catch him," Mrs. Cooke said, but that dumb hope didn't cheer me up. "Can you come out?" I whispered to Sheila. "I've got to talk to you alone."

Mr. Cooke took me by the elbow. "Come in and tell us exactly what happened. To tell the truth, I never trusted that man. We asked him to join the Chamber of Commerce, and you know what he said? That he didn't consider himself just from Glenfield—he said he was a citizen of the world! Citizen of the world, ha, ha—now I see what he meant! I wish you'd asked me before you got mixed up with him, Mike. I could have warned you, but I figured your dad ought to know—"

"I guess you didn't see your dad," Mrs. Cooke added. "Sheila tells us you haven't been living at home."

This was worse than I'd even imagined. Bad enough my own parents laying a guilt trip on me. "Excuse me," I told the Cookes, "I'd like to speak to Sheila alone."

They looked surprised and a little insulted, but I was determined to get my way, so I took Sheila's hand and led her out the door.

"Don't go away from the house!" her mom called. "I'll set an extra place at dinner, Mike!"

"Why don't you sit in the living room?" her dad shouted after us. "Plenty of places in the house where you two can be alone."

"No, thanks," I called back. I could tell Sheila was reluctant to follow, but she got into the car with me. When we got in, of course, Muttsy jumped up on Sheila and barked.

Sheila ducked. "What's she doing here?"

"She's coming with me, and so will you, I hope. This Burgess thing has gotten to me. I've got to get away. What do you say you come along?"

She blinked. "Where?"

"Someplace warm. We'll vacation first and then we'll see how we feel—"

"Mike, that's crazy. We can't!" She paused. "We'd miss Sunny and Billy's wedding!"

I had hoped not to have to play my last card, but now I decided I had to. I took both her hands in mine. "Yeah, let's miss theirs and have one of our own."

"Oh, Mike! I knew you'd come through!" Sheila's

cheeks were pink now. She threw her arms around me and kissed me. "As soon as school's over, okay? What date?"

"Wait, Sheila, I don't mean June." I pulled her closer. "I mean now."

"You can't have a nice wedding without time to plan it," she said.

I looked into her eyes. "You don't understand me. What I'm saying is, let's elope."

She shook her head. "I couldn't do it, not to my parents. My mother's been waiting since I was born to be mother of the bride."

Here I was asking her to marry me and she was worrying about her mother.

"Are you two coming in?" her mom called just then from the front steps. "You are staying for dinner, aren't you, Mike?"

"No, thanks," I shouted through the open window. "I can't!" Then I turned to Sheila. "If you're not going, if you're not saying yes, you'd better get out."

Her face crumpled. "Mike, what's happening?"

"Nothing. I asked you and you said no." I reached over and opened the door for her. Then I turned the key in the ignition.

Sheila hesitated for a second and then got out of the car. "This is insane. Where are you going, Mike, and *why*?"

"I want a fresh start, where nobody knows anything about me, not even that I won the lottery. I want to be anonymous."

"When will you be back?"

"I'm not sure. Want to change your mind and come?"

She burst into tears. "Mike, you know I can't!"

That's all I had to see to make me start up the car.

"Good-bye." Too bad for Sheila. She had had her chance. I stepped on the accelerator and drove across Glenfield. The next chance would be Ron's.

No sense bothering if he wasn't home, though. I stopped at the first outdoor telephone, plunked in two coins, and dialed.

"I. Ronald Schwartz here, I.R.S., not to be confused with the federal agency—"

"Ronnie, it's me. Glad you're home. I've got something major to ask you."

"Bronti! No, thanks, I don't want any deeds to Glenhaven townhouses, no matter how cheap. Just kidding. I *heard*, man. I'm really sorry you got taken. See what I meant now about Barry?"

"He wasn't in on it. He was just as dumb and unlucky as I was. Listen, that's water under the bridge. You still want to scout out a park location?"

"Are you kidding? Of course I do."

"I don't mean waiting for summer. I mean taking off now, bagging school."

A second's silence. "Why's that?"

"I need a vacation. The pressure's getting to me."

"What about graduating?"

"Who needs it?"

"Maybe *you* can get by without a diploma, but I'm still a poor slob. Hey, wait," Ronnie hooted, "a light bulb just lit up over my head. Idea! Make an offer on the whole abandoned Glenhaven Commons property. It'll probably be sold at auction or something. Borrow on your money that'll be coming. We'll build Bronti-saurus Park right here in Glenfield."

"Nononono, I want to get out of here. I don't want to be

reminded of Burgess! Come on, like we said—let's go on a long trip. I'll come over and pick you up. We'll hit the road tonight. I've still got ten thousand of this year's lottery money . . ."

"I think the money's curdling your brain, man. You're not taking a trip, you're running away—from what?"

"I'm just tired of all the hassles, everybody wanting something from me—my parents wanting me to be a good little investor, Sheila wanting me to settle down. You wanting me to be as obsessive as you are, Barry wanting to launch his career off me, Lingo wanting to stand in my shadow—it goes on and on."

"Poor little rich boy. No, wait—come on over here, I'm not mocking you. Bring some wonton and spareribs. We'll watch *Star Wars* for the fourteenth time and take your mind off the real world."

"You won't go with me?" I asked dully.

"Not until summer, man."

"All right. Tough on you, buddy. I'm going by myself." I hung up.

Walking back to my car, I felt almost glad that Ron had refused me. Who wanted to travel across the country with such a pigheaded guy? Always trying to be clever, always comparing my work unfavorably to his. I'd *rather* go by myself, like some hero in a Western film. "You and me, Mutts," I told her as I got behind the wheel again. Muttsy jumped from the back to the front, where she sat next to me. Who needed friends? Who wanted *humans*? Humans always wanted something from you. All Muttsy ever expected was a pat on the head.

Okay, we were off. I wasn't quite sure where to, but I liked the sense of freedom. I'd get on Route 80 and go west and stop somewhere for the night. Las Vegas! that's where I'd head for. Like Atlantic City but bigger. I'd quadruple my ten thousand. One thing first, though, I realized as I stopped for a light on Main Street. I hadn't eaten a thing since breakfast. It just so happened that there on the corner was good old Beefarama. And as luck would have it, when I pulled into the lot, I saw Lynne Carter coming out. I rolled down the window. "Hey, Lynne!"

"Mike, how are you?" She came running over, stuck her head in, and kissed me. "Your car—it's so beautiful! You told me about it, but this is the first time I'm seeing it. I've called you and left messages. Is everything okay? I haven't heard from you in ages!"

She didn't know about my recent goofs—good. "I've been busy. I was staying at Barry's." Wow, Lynne looked great. I hadn't seen her for so long I'd almost forgotten her sly smile.

"You've been at Barry's all this time? Still?"

"No, not anymore. Hey, where are you headed?" I asked.

"Home."

"Want to go someplace?"

"Okay."

"Good," I said, "get in. Let's go somewhere and have fun."

25

"Get in the back, Muttsy," I ordered as Lynne crawled into the front seat. "Meet my best friend," I said to her, nodding at Muttsy.

"She's great. Just the way I pictured her. I've heard so much about you!" Lynne petted Muttsy. "Hey, how come she isn't talking? In most of your cartoons she has the funniest lines."

"Keep your ears open. She'll probably come out with something. She's a lot nicer and funnier than *people* are. Feel like going somewhere?" I asked casually. By now I had a plan in mind, but I'd better get around to it gradually. "Somewhere exciting, how about it?"

"Depends where. My mother's expecting me."

"You could call her up, couldn't you?"

"Yes, I guess so. Why, where are you thinking of going?"

Pulling out of the parking lot, I glanced at her. "Have you ever felt like—getting away from it all?"

"Are you kidding? *Daily*. Especially *lately*. You're talking to the Prisoner of Beefarama."

"I have an idea," I said. "Let's drive to Las Vegas.

Wherever we stop tonight, you'll call your mom from there."

Lynne laughed. "She'd love that. So would Ptomaine Tom Nevelson. I'm working full time this coming week."

Driving down Main Street, I was silent. I had to watch how I handled this. I was determined to get out of Glenfield, but it wouldn't be much fun by myself. Now that Sheila and Ronnie had weaseled out on me, Lynne was the obvious person. I'd have to win her over slowly, though. "Are you hungry?" I asked.

"A little. I ate something at work, but you know how that is."

I pulled into the first parking space I saw. What should it be for my last meal in Glenfield, Gucci's Pizza or My Lin's Chinese? "It's okay, Mutts," I reassured her as we got out and locked the car. "We'll be right back, I swear. Don't worry, *we'll be back.*"

As Lynne and I stood between Gucci's and My Lin's, I felt this strong wave come over me of *What does anything matter? Who cares? What's the use?* I had thought money would solve everything, but all it had done so far was cause trouble. And what good was a piddling ten thousand? May as well blow it all. As I stood there, I noticed a sign in the window of Freed's Furs: SPRING SALE, PRICES SLASHED. Hey, buy my grandma her fur coat! I had meant to do it earlier. This would be my last chance before leaving Glenfield. "Lynne," I said, "before we eat, there's something important I've got to do."

What a brainstorm. Lynne had a ball, trying on furs and modeling them. She's the same height as my grandma but only about one third the width. They'd never met each other, but I had told so many stories about my grandma that Lynne got a kick out of helping me find the right coat. She twirled. "How's this? Too quiet and elegant?"

"Yeah, my grandma's into *flashy*. Try that one over there. How much is it?" I asked the saleswoman.

"Four thousand dollars."

Ten thousand, minus four thousand—wait, why count? The point was to *use it up*. We finally agreed on it, and I wrote a check, which meant I had six thousand dollars left. I arranged to have the coat sent the next day and wrote a card to include in the box that said, *"To Grandma, who knows how to enjoy life. Don't worry about me. Love, Mike."*

"Why should she worry about you?" Lynne asked as we left Freed's and walked toward Gucci's.

"She worries about everything." I wasn't ready to tell Lynne yet that I was planning to stay away for a while. I ended up ordering two Gucci Specials to go, and a major assortment from My Lin's. "Why so much?" Lynne asked. "Are you having a party?" Yeah, a farewell to Glenfield, as she would find out.

Buying takeout food was a good move. It meant we could get on the road faster. I figured once I had Lynne in the car, I could convince her to come away. "Just sit back and relax," I told her when we were ready to take off. "See, Mutts? We came back!" I started the engine and pulled out. "I'll drive for a little bit, and then we'll stop so we can eat."

Muttsy barked and Lynne reached over to calm her. "I'd like to know where I'm going. And I'd like to know what's wrong. You're acting so tense, and the fur coat—how come you bought it like that? And how come Muttsy's in the car?"

I turned off Main Street toward Route 80. "She likes to be with me."

"So do I," Lynne said, "but I also like to know where I'm going."

"For a ride."

She looked at me, annoyed. "Come on, tell me what's wrong. If you're not at Barry's anymore, where are you living?" She stretched to look over the seat. "And what're those cartons back there on the floor?"

"My mail."

"The fund letters? Are you moving?"

"You could say that." I nodded.

"Where to?"

I wasn't good at being a man of mystery. "I'm—all right, I'm leaving town."

"Oh? How come?"

"I've had some low blows since I saw you last. You heard about this shyster, Burgess?"

"Yes—"

I explained about giving him all my money and about how, because of my carelessness, Cummings had fallen through too.

"But just for *this* year," Lynne said. "Still, it's rotten. Even so, I don't see how it will help anything to leave Glenfield."

I stopped at a light. "I'll be an *unknown* again in some other place. No one'll be calling, or expecting things from me, or bossing me around, or following me."

"Is that what's most important to you, being anonymous?"

"*Yeah.*"

"I thought you were enjoying the attention."

"I was in the beginning. But now everyone's watching me and thinking *He sure botched things up.*" While I was talking, I worked the pizza carton open and started to pull out a slice of it.

Lynne helped me. "If you stayed here, couldn't you *un*-botch some of those things?" she asked.

I bit into the pizza, burned my mouth, and almost lost control of the steering wheel. "When my next lottery check comes, maybe, but that's nine months away."

"You mean, the only way you can see to solve problems now is by spending a lot of money?"

"Come on, Lynne, lay off the questions."

"Okay." She looked out the window. "Okay, let's change the subject. Where are you taking me?"

"I was serious about going to Vegas."

She raised her eyebrows but didn't say anything.

"Now I'm thinking, let's just have a good time. I've got six thousand bucks left. I want to spend it. It's too little to do anything important with. Let's just drive, all night maybe, and stop whenever we want."

"*We?*" Lynne gave me a hard look. "If I get a vote, and I certainly hope I do, I'd like to stop now before the food gets cold."

At that point my slice of pizza slipped and landed upside down. "Damn! Okay, I've got an idea where we can stop and eat." I turned at the corner and stepped on the accelerator. "I want to show you something anyway." I left the main road and took one that wound past a row of nice farms. The sun was going down now and the sky was purplish pink.

"This is pretty," Lynne said after we'd driven for several miles. "Where are we?"

"One-half hour from downtown Glenfield." I pulled into the deserted parking lot.

Lynne sat up and glanced at the sign. "Oh! So this is Glenhaven Commons." She took a long look at the hills around us and at the abandoned equipment. "It's a fantastic location. I see why you're fuming mad."

I got out of the car and put Muttsy on her leash. "Feel like walking?" I asked Lynne.

"Sure. I'll carry the pizzas. Is this what you wanted to show me—what you almost owned?"

"Yeah." I got my gym bag out of the trunk and stuffed the Chinese food in it. Then we walked across the lot toward the swimming pool. POOL WILL BE OPEN TO RESIDENTS MEMORIAL DAY. *Sure.* The bottom was covered with stagnant water. "Over here is where my units would have been." I showed Lynne the spot. "This one was almost finished. I was going to rent it to Sheila's cousin. Over here"—I pointed—"they were going to excavate for two more." I thought about standing in Burgess's office feeling as important as Yertle the Turtle. Suddenly I remembered where Yertle ended up—in the mud, just like me.

"It's really sad." Lynne kept staring. "Maybe they'll catch Burgess some day. Have you spoken to the people who are investigating?"

I shrugged. "What's the use?" Muttsy pulled me toward the entrance of the almost finished unit then, where I tried to open the door but found it was locked. I motioned for Lynne to follow me. "The spa building doesn't have doors yet. Let's go over there. We can sit inside and eat."

Stopping to let Muttsy pee, I watched Lynne walk around a pile of cinder blocks. Then we went together, with Muttsy pulling me, into the spa.

"This would have been beautiful," Lynne said. "Look at the skylights, all the light in here, even now. The walls are so smooth and white." She found an empty packing crate and put the pizzas down. Then we upended a couple of cinder blocks, so that we'd have something to sit on. "Still hungry?" Lynne asked.

"Yeah." I unpacked the ribs and fried rice. "Hungry for revenge on Burgess."

She held out a slice of pizza. "You can't forget for a minute, can you?"

"I'd love to get my hands on him. Maybe I'll go on a manhunt."

"Wouldn't that be frustrating?" Lynne nibbled her pizza. "The whole D.A.'s office has been working, and they don't have a lead yet. Besides, say you found him in South America or someplace, what would you do with him?"

"I don't know," I admitted, tearing off another slice of pizza. "But you can't let people like Burgess get away. Hell, it's not fair!"

"Not much is fair in life."

"Quit being so philosophical!" I grunted. "What do you mean, not much is fair? Are you saying it's not fair that I won two million bucks and really poor people are still poor?"

Lynne looked surprised. "Come on, Mike. That's not what I mean. I don't happen to be crazy about lotteries, frankly. I think money's nicer to have if you've earned it, but lotteries give a lot of people hope, so I don't think they're bad. Do you feel guilty about winning?"

"Yes—*no!* No, I don't feel guilty! I'm just deep-down angry! Having money's supposed to be fun! And I'm going to make sure it *is.*" I crammed my mouth full of pizza and reached in my gym bag. "Eat, Lynne, enjoy yourself!" I handed her an egg roll and a sparerib. "Look, come away from here with me. You said you're thinking every day of making a getaway. I've only got six thousand right now, but I can borrow on my next year's check—"

"Mike, sit down."

By this time I was all hopped up. "I don't want to sit down! I want to get out of here . . . start a new life someplace. Will you come with me?"

Lynne shook her head.

She wouldn't? When I heard that, I felt a new wave of pain. Nobody really understood me—not my parents, not Sheila, Ron, or Amy. Not Lynne, in this moment of crisis, even though she always had before. Okay, *by myself* I'd go away. I stood, pizza in one hand, Chinese food in the other, staring in fury at the bare, white walls which seemed to be mocking me. Here, before I went—*Here, Burgess, this is for you!* Stepping up to the smooth wallboard, I hurled pizza and fried rice. Then I went for the rest of the pizza and smeared it piece by piece on the wall. I made swirls of tomato sauce and created a 3-D effect with mushrooms. Next, dunking my fingers in mustard and soy, I wrote BURGESS IS A LOUSY THIEF.

"Go on," Lynne encouraged me, while Muttsy licked at the dripping mural. "Get it out of your system. We'll call it *Bronti's Italian-Oriental Revenge!*"

Maybe she did understand me a little. I doused a sparerib with some reddish stuff and used it like a brush to draw a caricature of Burgess. I stuck on some Chinese-noodle prison bars and gave him a mozzarella mustache. Then, as long as there were any sauces left, I moved from one wall to another, painting caricatures, and little cartoons, and slogans like BURN, BURGESS, BURN.

When my "paint" ran out, it was almost dark. I could

hardly see to sign my murals. "What's that?" Lynne asked in a whisper, and Muttsy let out a suspicious growl. There was the sound of a motor far off. Headlights shone in the distance. "Let's get out of here," Lynne said, and I decided she had the right idea.

"Take me home, please," she said, after we were safely back in my car again.

I turned on the motor and headed for Glenfield.

She looked up. "What are you going to do?"

"After I drop you off? Take my best girl to dinner—stake Mutts to some Alpo, that is."

"That's more like it," Lynne said. "I think you're on your way to getting it back."

"My money?"

"Your sense of humor."

"You think I lost it?"

"For a while there. *Don't.*" She nudged me gently. "It's worth a lot more than two and a half million bucks. Seriously, what are you going to do now?"

"Finish off my last six thousand."

"On what?"

"On the fund people I've been stringing along. I don't need six grand myself. How about helping me, like you said you would. Read me some of those letters there in the back."

During the ride home, Lynne turned on the light and read me a bunch of letters. " *'Dear Mike, Want to buy a racehorse?'* "

"Ugh."

" *'Dear Mike Bronti, I need a new wheelchair . . . '* "

"Keep looking for ones like that," I said. "Let's mail out the checks tonight, before I change my mind." When we got back to Glenfield, we went to Lynne's house, and I made out checks to twenty-five people. Lynne wrote the addresses and sealed the envelopes, and my balance was down to thirty-one dollars. "Easy come, easy go," I said. "Thanks a lot, Lynne—for putting up with me. I'm feeling better about everything, at least for the time being."

"Are you going home now?"

"No"—I kissed her cheek—"one more stop."

"It's after midnight."

"Yeah, well—this is something else I've been putting off long enough."

I said good night, I'd see her soon. Then I mailed the envelopes at the Glenfield Post Office. Now the last errand . . . make sure she would accept my checks. After stopping to get Muttsy food, I got back into the Camaro. Then I drove, with the hope that Amy wouldn't mind having a visitor arrive so late.

26

Here it is, June, suddenly, the last week of school, five months since I won the lottery. And where am I—in Las Vegas? Tracking down Burgess across oceans and mountains? No, I'm in New Jersey, specifically where, I'll leave you to guess. Here are some clues: the heat's on, there's lots of action, there's the jingle of coins and tinkle of glasses, happy voices are ringing out . . . Meanwhile, let me bring things up to date.

I barged into Murray very late, the night that I went down to see Amy. She didn't mind, though—she was staying awake anyway for an All-Night Vigil for Hunger Relief. She was happy to see me in spite of all the times I'd postponed my visits, and she agreed that the next day she'd go out and cash the checks I'd made out to her group. What a bunch. Most of them looked as if they could use a good meal at my grandma's. I took the liberty of inviting them. I was sure my grandma would want me to. When I reluctantly told Amy about losing so much of my money, she tried to make me feel better by saying, "Well, I hope Burgess is hiding out in some South American country, so at least he's helping to stimulate their weak economy."

"Meanwhile, I'm down to zero until I get my next year's check," I told her. "I gave my last six thousand bucks to twenty-five people who wrote in."

"Good, I'm proud of you." She actually hugged me. "See, you *are* a good person. Maybe we *are* blood brother and sister after all."

Since the night I almost left Glenfield, a lot of things have happened. I'm mulling them over now, as I stand here with a brush in my hand. I've been commissioned, on the basis of my past experience, to paint a small comic display. Where? Oh, you'll find out—in this mystery place where I am. The day after I did the spa murals, I went back to Glenhaven Commons and took some photographs. It's a good thing I did, too, because a couple of weeks later there was a headline in the *Independent:* COUNTY TAKES OVER BURGESS LAND; GLENHAVEN STRUCTURES MAY BE RAZED. The article said that the half-finished spa had already been the target of an "ambitious and original graffiti artist." I cut out the article and saved it, along with my lottery clippings. What I'm hoping is that somebody will realize what a treasure they have there and decide to preserve the spa as a county art museum.

Speaking of the *Independent,* they've been wasting a lot of ink on Sean Burgess. Every day there's a new story about where he might be hiding out. The most recent one reported rumors that he'd been seen snorkeling in the Bahamas. I can't picture it, but of course I was wrong about the guy before. Meanwhile, Barry, good old Barry—I see him pretty often in this place where I am right now. He comes in to socialize and to drop a few bucks. He's working for Glen Mutual now, bragging about the killing he's going to make in insurance. To shut him up, I've promised to buy a policy from him when my next check comes through in seven months.

Okay, who else? My bodyguard Lingo, who's still being as loyal as ever. Wherever I go next year, whatever I do, he'll *be* there, if I want him to be. Burgess would never have gypped me, he claims, if he, Lingo, hadn't ever left sight of me. I love the guy like I love Muttsy, and I don't want to hurt his feelings, but I can't go through my whole life with Lingo shadowing me.

On to Ronnie. What's happening with Schwartz? Hold it a minute, while I call him. I shouldn't be making personal calls on this line, but—wait till I put down this brush. "Hello, Ron?"

"You have reached 201-555-1731. If you are a money-obsessed, fame-crazed, so-called friend who's ashamed of yourself, leave your humble apology at the sound of the tone."

"Look, I'm busy, old buddy, too busy to think up a comeback. I'm bringing some spicy chicken and spring rolls over to your place later on. I'll wait till then to tell you to go soak your head in duck sauce."

Ron still says once in a while that my money's making me crazy. Of course he's saying it less often now that I'm back to being broke. Sometimes I see him drawing a new amusement park feature and I hear him sighing, as if he's thinking, *We could be involved in this already.* He thinks Barry brainwashed me into buying the townhouses, and he can't understand why I don't hold a grudge. But giving Burgess the money was *my own fault.* I did it because I *liked* Glenhaven Commons. Plus I was trying to please a few people and prove how smart I was to my dad. The truth is that lately I don't see Barry nearly as much as I used to. I guess our values are different. He's out hustling insurance and I'm here pursuing my art.

Speaking of art, Ron's starting Cummings in September. It's going to be hard seeing him go to California without me. My chances of being chosen from the Cummings waiting list are one-in-four at this point. Even if I do get in, the cross-country trip with Ron will have to wait. I'm finally facing reality. That's why I'm standing here right now, painting this figure on the wall, for money. I owe the tax-men a few thousand. They started breathing down my neck at the end of April. They'd been writing me letters that I found in my cartons of mail.

Mail is still coming in, including a big bill charged to my credit cards before I got around to reporting them stolen. With luck, the muggers will be traced, caught, and arrested for credit-card fraud. Most of my mail, though, has been much nicer—thank-you notes from the people I sent checks to. Amy's group, for instance, wrote to thank me for my moral support as well as my bucks. They're hoping I'll go to Murray next year (I was accepted!), and I might, if I don't get into Cummings. I'm still betting on Cummings, though. I've beat worse odds than theirs before.

Hey, big news—Sunny and Billy are married! They found a decent garden apartment, and they're eating hot dogs and tuna in order to pay their landlord a high rent. They're really happy, in spite of the fact that an exciting evening for them these days is watching wrestling on cable TV. Just goes to show that you can be contented without being rich.

The wedding was a blast. Luckily all their relatives held

off arguing for as long as it lasted. I looked pretty good in my baby-blue tux, if I do say so myself. Sheila's parents kept winking at me significantly through the whole ceremony, and they practically helped Sheila catch the bridal bouquet, but, surprisingly, Sheila has cooled off lately about weddings. She says she wants to finish Glenfield Community before she takes the big step.

I'm relieved. I'm not ready to settle down with one woman. Sheila and I are still seeing each other, but she met some guys at the G.C. orientation, and I can't say I'm jealous. I'm too busy these days to be serious about a female—working on this mural, giving depositions against Burgess, getting ready for graduation. . . . Hey, guess what—I passed my math final by one lucky point!

I did better in my other courses. I got a B plus in English after writing a paper on "Attitudes Toward Money in Chekhov's 'The Bet.'" Ever since my English teacher, the Monk, heard about my trouble with Burgess, he's been putting quotes on the board that are supposed to be good advice: "If you make money your god, it will plague you like the devil" (Fielding); and "Money is a good servant, but a dangerous master" (Bonhours). I came back at him by attaching this quote from Samuel Johnson to my paper: "No man but a blockhead ever wrote except for money."

You're probably wondering how things are going between me and my family. I had some rough times with my dad the first few days after the Burgess mess. He would yell at me one minute and then feel bad and try to comfort me. He was angry at himself, I think, for letting me make mistakes on my own. "Don't worry, it's only money," he'd say. And then *But why did you give him two big checks like that?* And finally, "It's water under the bridge, Mike. Don't let it bother you, okay?"

I'm getting used to my dad. His good side always wins out in the end. I figure by the time he's gained confidence and success managing Bronti and Father Realty, he'll probably be a great guy. I'm hoping he'll do that, help me manage my income, while I learn about other things. I've already suggested that our first purchase should be those white elephant buildings of his. Ron loves the idea of turning them into commercial haunted houses.

My mom, by the way, was upset by my farewell letter when she found it—the one I left in my room when I intended to take off. "I agree, you *should* be on your own as soon as you can afford it," she said, "but let's cut out these dramatic departures! Next time, come tell us you want to leave and we'll help you find a place."

So things have been going pretty well at home. I won't be there too much longer. I'll be out at Cummings or down at Murray, on my own, like I've wanted to be. Now that I'm leaving and my parents are in favor of it, it's a little sad, I've admitted to Lynne. "It's nice that you feel that way," she says. "It means you're close to your family."

I am. I agree. I was stupid to think of running out on them. I still need them a lot of the time and they still need me. For instance, just the other day, I was here, working on this mural, and my mom called me from home. "You don't have Muttsy there with you, do you?"

"No, no dogs allowed. Why?"

She sucked in her breath. "She wasn't at the door when I came home, so I searched the house." My mom paused. "Then I put out her dinner and," her voice cracked, "it's still here!"

My throat tightened. "Was anybody in the house?"

"The cleaning service was here today—"

Muttsy's worst fears of dognapping had finally come

true. "I'll be right home," I told her. "In the meantime, call and demand her back!"

"Dad's out looking for her," my mom said. "Grandma's on her way over here with fresh meatballs. She swears if Muttsy's alive she'll smell them, wherever she is."

Well, Grandma's plan actually worked. As soon as she arrived and set out the meatballs, Muttsy began to bark and scratch like mad. The cleaning people had accidentally shut her in the closet upstairs. Afterward, when the crisis was over and we were sitting around the supper table, I said, "Let's drop the cleaning service. Who needs them? I'll clean my own room from now on."

My parents looked at each other in disbelief.

"I'll even start doing my own laundry."

My mom flashed me a smile. "Are you sorry I did your laundry on that day five months ago?"

"No!"

"Me, neither." Grandma jiggled my arm and planted one of her lipstick kisses on my cheek. "Otherwise I'd still be wearing that sick rat instead of my beautiful coat!"

"What do you think, Lou?" my mom asked my dad. "Do you think we'd be better off if the ticket had gotten lost forever?"

My dad glanced up from the *Independent*. "I'm not sure. Too early to tell. Ask me again in twenty years."

I can't believe I'll ever be sorry about winning the money. So there've been some problems, but look at it this way: I've got nineteen more times to get it right. That's where the luck comes in—not that I'm so rich but that I'll keep getting lots of new chances, to go places, and help people out, and get good at something like drawing.

Which brings us back to where I am now, my mystery

location. I'm standing with Lynne, talking and laughing like we usually do. When neither one of us is busy with our regular duties, she watches me work on my current masterpiece—the life-size Beefarama Bunny that Nevelson asked me to paint on the wall. Yeah, that's right. I'm back on the job, under the sign of the big red B. A comedown, you say? Nah, I don't think of it like that. Aside from making money to pay my taxes, I see Lynne almost every day. And besides, this job is only temporary.

So that's where I am, still basically happy, the way I was before all this happened. Lynne keeps telling me that winning money doesn't change most people very much. If you're miserable when you're poor, you'll probably be miserable as a rich guy. I have a feeling that if I've learned anything, it's that the truth was in that fortune cookie I got at Ronnie's. How was it worded? Something like *"Happiness is found in work."* I don't mean serving burgers at Beefarama. I mean working at something you really care about, the way I care about my drawings when they're turning out right. One thing I know is, I'd give the rest of my two million to be as good an artist as Ronnie. On the other hand, if I never make it as a cartoonist, I'm not going to sit around and mope. I'll try to be like Muttsy and take what comes to me. I'll try to be like my grandma and enjoy life. I'll be like Lynne and be interested in people. And if I happen to be rich on top of that—well, it won't hurt!

ROBIN F. BRANCATO earned her B.A. in creative writing from the University of Pennsylvania and received her M.A. from the City College of New York. She has written several award-winning books for young adults, including *Winning*, and she believes the single biggest influence on her writing was the 12 years she spent teaching English and journalism in a New Jersey high school. Ms. Brancato currently lives in Teaneck, New Jersey, with her husband and two sons.